D0667405
LIBRARY
MURRAY STATE UNIVERSITY

YOU MUST BREAK OUT SOMETIMES

YOU MUST BREAK OUT SOMETIMES

and other stories by

THOMAS OWEN BEACHCROFT

Short Story Index Reprint Series

BOOKS FOR LIBRARIES PRESS
FREEPORT, NEW YORK

First Published 1937
Reprinted 1970

STANDARD BOOK NUMBER:
8369-3377-X

LIBRARY OF CONGRESS CATALOG CARD NUMBER:
75-113648

PRINTED IN THE UNITED STATES OF AMERICA

CONTENTS

Mother is so Wilful 11
You Must Break Out Sometimes 23
The Three Priests 57
Joey's Law Case 79
The Young Against the Old 99
Old Hard 112
May-Day Celebrations 128
Busting Him One 146
The Stoker 158
If You Can't be Good, be Cautious 177
A Job at Staedtler's 194
We were Lovers too 213
I'll Spoil Your Pretty Face 218
Bees have Wars, too 245

'My people humble people who expect
Nothing.'

THE WASTE LAND

MOTHER IS SO WILFUL

'So long, mother,' said Will. 'You're all ready, aren't you?'

'I'm ready,' said Mother. 'Been ready all day, my son. It's Ronnie that's keeping us waiting now.'

'Well, I'm just going up the road to see if I can meet him,' said Will. 'Then we'll start. I'll be back in a couple of shakes.'

'Don't you fret over me,' said Mother. 'I shall be here. I'm used to sitting alone.'

Will went out of the garden, with its profusion of vegetables and cottage flowers, and set off up the road. Twice before he was out of sight he turned round to wave and smile at his mother: but her eyes did not follow him or give any sign that she was watching. He strolled on for about a mile, till he passed the other houses in the village, and came to a fork in the road where there was a signpost marked 'Five miles to Sanditon'.

He could see the road winding away up the hill in the distance towards Sanditon. Presently a car appeared, and in another few minutes drew up beside him. It was new and small and shining. His brother Ronnie climbed out.

'Well,' said Ronnie, 'here I am, Will. Is she all right and ready?'

'She's ready,' said Will. 'Been ready hours.'

'That's good,' said Ronnie, and nodded. 'Well there's nothing to keep us now. Get in, Will. We'll take her along in the car at once.'

Will fitted himself in beside his brother.

'I hope she'll come in the car,' he said.

'Don't you get putting her up to things,' said Ronnie. 'Just like you, Will. Why shouldn't she come in the car?'

'Well I don't know,' said Will. 'She's taking it all a bit funny. You might expect that.'

'The less said the better.' Ronnie let the clutch in and they moved off. 'I'm sure it's the right thing for her. Now she's all alone here, and we shall both be living at Sanditon. The new house looks a treat, Will. Wait till you see it. She'll have running hot water in the kitchen with a double sink, and a patent cooker. And she can pick any girl in the village to come and help her. She'll have the time of her life, as soon as she's settled in.'

'Look,' said Will. 'There she is: she's been sitting in her sun-house all day, pretending she's not thinking about it at all.'

The two men got out of the car and paused to look at her for a few moments before she saw them.

Mother's sun-house was a flimsy erection run up one afternoon fifteen years ago when they were still in their teens. It was simply a couple of match-board sides, without a roof, anchored into the soft earth of a flower-bed against one side of the cottage.

Flowering creepers now grew all over it and had turned it into a canopy of tangled greenery, jewelled in turn with yellow jasmine blossoms and pink and white dog roses. Nasturtiums massed themselves round its sheltered corners, and two giant sunflowers grew up beside it turning their yellow-bearded negro faces to the sunshine.

Here in her favourite seat, which kept out all the wind and let in all the sun, mother sat whenever she was not busy; her eye roving round the garden; her brown wizened hands flying over her knitting. She seemed to her two sons the most indefatigable old woman in the world.

Ronnie called, and pushed open the garden gate. Mother put her work away with her spectacles in a brown paper bag without looking up.

'Here I am, mother,' said Ronnie. 'Are you ready?' He saw her eye travel for a moment to the motor car; but she made no comment.

'I'm ready,' she said. 'I've got my bonnet on my head and all. I shan't go in the house again. I don't like to see it all looking so empty.'

'I've got all your furniture set out in the new house,' said Ronnie. 'It looks a treat.'

Mother said nothing.

'Well,' said Ronnie briskly. 'There's my little car, mother. Don't you like it?'

Mother nodded.

'Would you like to sit in the front with me, or at the back with Will?'

There was a long, threatening silence. Mother

drew a deep breath and compressed her lips tightly together. Then she said:

'You know full well, Ronnie, I never rode in no motor cars yet; and I'm not going to now.'

'Ah,' said Will. 'That's right, mother. I was afraid you mightn't like it. We'll soon find some other way.'

'You'd better,' she said. 'Here have I been sitting an hour or more waiting for you two boys to take me over, and now you bring a motor car. Well I'd better go back and sit some more.'

She returned to the sun-house. Ronnie made an angry gesture to Will to be silent, and he went over and stood close to his mother's chair.

'But, mother dear——' he said.

'Don't you get dearing me.' She was already at her knitting again.

'But look, mother. I've had that car for months now. I go everywhere in it.'

'It may suit you all right, my boy: but it don't suit me. Cars is for the young.'

Ronnie was a successful shopkeeper in Sandiiton. He was used to persuading people. He felt sure he could win her over.

Will wandered away. He was not happy about the line his elder brother was taking. In a quarter of an hour he came back and drew up at the gate of the cottage with a pleasing jingle of harness and clatter of hooves. He had borrowed old Mr. Thurston's mare, Polly, and dogcart: the last dogcart in the village.

He left Polly to stand in the shafts and came into the cottage garden. He found Ronnie still talking, and his mother knitting hard.

'Say what you like, Ronnie,' he heard her say at length, 'you can't talk me into thinking I want to go into that car of yours.'

Ronnie made an exasperated exclamation and pushed his hat on to the back of his head.

'But mother——' he began for the sixth time.

At this moment Will came forward.

'It's all right, mother,' he said. 'Don't worry, Ronnie. I've got old Thurston to lend me his dog-cart. We'll go in that. Come on, mother.'

Mother looked up the garden and glared at a cat. She was not attending, it seemed, to her sons or the dogcart. She said almost abstractedly:

'I saw you bring old Thurston's dogcart up, Will. And I'm not going in that tittupy thing, neither.'

Will made no answer.

'That cat,' said mother. 'I believe it got one of my young chickens last week. No, Will, I should look a pretty sight morrissing round the country in old Thurston's dogcart at my age. And you'd tip me out like as not.'

'You'd much better come in the car,' said Ronnie.

'I could bring round the milk float,' said Will. 'But I thought you used to like riding in that dog-cart.'

'Like it,' said Mother, 'you're going zaney, Will. I never rode in that dogcart in my life.'

'Surely, mother——'

'Now you let me speak, son. I never rode in that dogcart in my life. And I never rode in any dogcart belonging to anyone. And now you set me thinking, I never rode in any cart. So don't start talking to me about dogcarts and milk floats. I never rode in anything as far as I recall, in all my born and blessed days, and I ain't going to begin now. Seventy-five years my legs 'as been good enough to get about on, and I ain't going to start riding abroad like all these fat good-for-nothing young trollops. I've walked the bettermost part of my days already, and I shall walk them out now. My left leg's a bit funny but it's good enough to get me over to Sanditon once more. I shall walk. That's what I shall do.'

As she finished talking she put her knitting and spectacles back into the brown paper bag once more, and stood up.

'Out of my way, you two great men,' she said: and carefully turning her eyes aside from the car and from Polly, who was now pulling brambles out of the hedge, she set off into the heat of the afternoon.

She was a small, wiry old woman, bent, but unsubdued; and her step was lame but brisk. For a moment Ronnie and Will stared at her, uncertain what to say or do. Then they hurried off after her.

'What did you want to bring that damn dogcart for?' said Ronnie. 'See what you've made her do.'

'It was you arguing about the car that's done it,' said Will. 'We'll never get her out of this fancy now.'

At the end of the village they caught her up, and began to walk one on each side of her.

'You're a silly old woman,' said Ronnie, loudly and angrily. 'You'll make yourself ill. That's what you'll do.'

She answered in a very quiet, icy voice.

'A nice way to talk to your old mother. A clout over the 'ear-'ole would do you good.'

Will guffawed at this. Ronnie, exploding with anger, turned away, and went back to attend to Polly and the dog-cart.

'That boy Ronnie,' mother said. 'Bellocking out at me like that! I know they all think the world of 'im at Sanditon, but I won't stand it.'

After a little while Will offered her his arm, and was thankful that she took it, and leant on it heavily. Her brisk pace soon died away, and they made slow progress.

'I ain't so good at walking nowadays,' she said. 'But I shall get there! all in good time."

It was now about three o'clock, and the sun was glaring down with full strength. Ronnie and Will had planned to have their mother comfortably installed in Ronnie's new house by tea-time. But at a quarter to five Will found himself still 2 miles away. Mother's pace grew slower and slower; and for the last half-hour she had said nothing at all.

'I'll tell you what, mother,' he said.' I want to

take a stone out of my shoe ; so we'll sit on this nice shady bank, and you can have a rest.'

She sat down thankfully and gave a sigh. Will was shocked to see how pale and ill she looked, and unhappy pictures began to come before his mind. It was a bad thing for her to be uprooted from the cottage where she had lived for so long. Suppose she never reached that new house at all. He knew he ought to prevent her walking any further ; but he had no idea how to do it.

'There's no need to go looking at me all a-gloar,' she said severely. 'Give me ten minutes to rest ; and I shall be fine.'

At this very moment they heard a hoot ; and Ronnie's car turned a corner and drew up beside them.

He had brought Will's wife with him, and a good tea packed in a basket. There were plenty of tasty sandwiches, and smoking hot tea in thermos flasks.

After a cup, mother began to recover her spirits. She made a good meal, and her sprightliness came back to her. Ronnie was all attention to her, and half an hour or more passed very quickly and pleasantly.

Presently, Ronnie said 'It's nearly six. Won't you come the rest of the way in the car, mother? You've practically done it now.'

'No,' said mother. 'No thank you, Ronnie. I know you mean it kindly, so don't take me amiss. I've never rode in anything in my life, and I'm going to do this on my own legs. Once I get there I shan't do no more journeying. I'm too old to start riding.'

'But, Mother,' said Will. 'You must have ridden some time or other. Surely, you've been in a train?'

'No,' said mother. 'Never.'

'Then in the hay-carts when you were a child.'

'No.'

'What about a perambulator?'

'We never had them things *then*.'

'Well, on your wedding day?'

'There wasn't no call. We were too close to the church. Now don't you boys start arguing with me again. I'm going to walk it all now.'

This time it was Will who drove the car. An hour later mother entered her new house, exhausted, but smiling on the arm of her eldest son. After she had rested, and Will and his wife had joined them again for a friendly supper in the kitchen, they set their chairs on the tiled verandah outside, and the men lit their pipes.

A peaceful, brooding quiet had now fallen; and the summer dusk was closing round them, soft, and brown, and scented. Though Ronnie's house and garden were new, the little town of Sanditon was all old, and they looked across the garden to the square church tower, and the rich outlines of oaks and towering elms soft as black velvet in the night air. They breathed in the scents of grass, of yellow night primroses, and of the earth deliciously refreshed by the evening dew. Both men were thinking the same: and their thoughts were a little sad, but peaceful.

'Well, Mother,' said Ronnie. 'I think we'll make this garden pretty good for you in a little while. Wait till you see it in the afternoon sun, and we'll plan just where to build you a new sun-house.'

Mother nodded.

'I shall be well enough here,' she said. 'And I ain't going to spend all my time sitting about, either. I'm glad I comed here on my own legs, too: now I can say as I never rode a yard in all my days.'

They listened, and she ran on:

'And that's more than most women can say, I'll bet. I'll get abroad in this garden and up the street. And none of your nasty bath chairs. When my legs give out I'll get crutches; and when I can't use them no more, you can put me to bed, and let me lie. And then you can say "She never rode on wheels: her own two stumps was all she asked and needed" and you can put that on my gravestone.'

Silence fell, and in the darkness, their minds ran on from what she had been saying.

'Ronnie,' she said, 'and Will; I want to ask you two boys something particular.'

'Yes,' said Ronnie.

'There will be another journey,' she said. 'And I shan't be able to walk it.'

They nodded. The countless leaves whispered and sighed in the night air.

'And I ain't going to do *that* on wheels either: do you hear me?'

'Yes.'

'Promise me?'

'Yes.'

'Honest to God.'

'Yes, mother.'

Will and Ronnie stared at each other.

'How will you do it?'

'I don't quite know, mother. We'll manage somehow. Hadn't ever thought of it.'

'Well think now. And you, too, Will. Can you carry—Can you carry——?'

Her voice broke off. She failed to make her mouth say what they could carry. Ronnie said nothing. It was Will who answered tapping out his pipe on the pavement.

'Not alone, we couldn't. Not us two.'

'But there'll be enough men there,' she said. 'There'll be plenty besides you.'

'Yes.'

'I'll tell you what,' she went on, her voice brightening up. 'You have some handles put on. Plenty of good, strong handles. Not just one at each end: but several good ones down each side. You get 'em to do that for you.'

'That's it, mother.'

'Well that's *that*,' she said with great decision. 'I wonder why neither of you two couldn't have thought of that for me. I never set out to be a scholar like our Ronnie. Now before we say good-night, you boys would like a drink. I saved up a little of my money last month, and I've brought over a bottle of whisky for Ronnie, as it's my first night in his new 'ouse.'

In another five minutes the occasion became cheerful and festive. Will made the whiskies good and strong. Mother took some whisky herself and proposed her own health.

'Here's to your old mother,' she said. 'As never rode on wheels once the whole way from the cradle to the grave—and proud of it, too!'

YOU MUST BREAK OUT SOMETIMES

They say the old-fashioned doss-houses are all going, and giving place to these municipally controlled and licensed places. It's thought to be a great gain in hygiene : but the war taught us a lot about fighting parasites, and bugs no longer lead their old easy life.

Anyhow, Happy Jack's is as clean a place as anyone need worry to find. And most men would agree that there are worse smells to meet when your spirits are down than bugs : and one is the smell of official rules and regulations working hand in glove with the police. Name? Married? Any money? Where been? Where living? Where last employed? Take your clothes off and leave them here. Yes, we're going to bake them, you lousy beast; and turning the key in the lock quietly and silently behind you : sign here : and here : here's your passing-in ticket. You'll get your passing-out one to-morrow when the superintendent's seen you.

Well meant? So's a snake bite well meant; but not to the man that gets bitten.

But Happy Jack's isn't a doss-house of the official sort at all. It's friendly. Happy never let a copper or any sort of official through his door without passing the word round first, and keeping them on the doorstep for about five minutes. He had reasons of his own perhaps for holding them off.

And then in his unspeaking, heavy sort of way,

Happy hindered them and stood in their way the whole time. He hung round them like a mournful elephant; sixteen stone of him: calling them 'Sir', wheezing at them, and misunderstanding everything they said. Happy had a face like a gigantic bloodhound, with red eyes and drooping pouches under them: and sagging folds of flesh that hung down and made him look as if he were going to cry.

So ran Dave Barker's thoughts as he dragged along his exhausted limbs and rain-sodden clothes. He looked up at the doors of the casual ward—the end of his day's walk. The winter twilight drew round him like a cold, damp cloak, making him shiver.

This casual ward had an evil name. There were two or three men sitting on the bank outside. They would not be admitted for half an hour yet. Dave was wet through, and aching in every limb. His bones felt soaked and rotten and numbed with the rain.

Then he thought again of Happy Jack's down in the town three miles away. He began to see the fire that Happy always kept going: the big, blazing fire he could push his way up to. Happy's wasn't the cheapest sort of doss; it cost a bob. Dave had one and tuppence—and another two days' walk before him. But the fire and friendliness at Happy Jack's struck him as the thing he needed most in the world.

He dragged himself along for a mile more. Then he gave it up and took the tram down into the town just as dusk was coming on. The people in the tram looked at him : the conductor seemed a bit surprised to find he had got the twopence for the fare. The tram banged and rattled on, and he fell asleep.

'You get off here,' the conductor said to him. 'Your twopence is up.'

Dave got out into the rain, and the tram went on.

He took to the back streets. He had only been to Happy's once before. He buttoned up his soaked jacket and pulled up his trousers. You couldn't ask a bobby the way to a place like Happy's. You couldn't ask anyone.

Dave wandered on. Suddenly he found the place : simply a door in a dirty brick wall. It was quite dark now, and the street was small and ill-lighted. He lifted the latch and pushed : the door opened. The first door led into a stone passage-way. There was another door at the end. He pushed this and it opened too. At once he was in the main room of Happy's doss.

This was a very simply constructed place. The floor was the broken, pitted concrete of an outside yard, surrounded on all sides by bare brick walls. It had been roofed over with corrugated iron carried on iron posts. It was a rough job—but it kept all the draughts out.

As he stepped through the door, Dave walked into a delicious red warmth. There was no light —only the glow of a leaping fire against the far wall. There was a second stove in the middle of the floor. The whole place was blinking in the half light of the fire. Dave stood uncertainly by the door. Dark shapes of half a dozen men were grouped round each fire. Some had dragged up mattresses and benches to the warmth. There were a few more benches and trestle-top tables about, and beds and mattresses in the dark corners.

Dave went up and stood near the open fire. One or two of the men looked up at him. There wasn't much talk. Dave stood behind, and presently his clothes began to steam, and the warmth began to creep through. After a while he crossed to the far wall where he opened a door and looked through. He shut this, and looked round for another door, which he soon found.

The other men looked round with interest as he opened this.

'Hey!' came a voice. Dave turned back, with his hand on the door, but made no answer.

'Stay here. He'll be up to take your bob. You can't go through there.'

A man came up to him in the gloom and looked into his face.

'I'm going down to see Mike.'

'Do you know him?'

'Yes. He's a friend of mine. I've been here before.'

'When did you come?'

'Eighteen months ago,' said Dave. 'It's all right. I'm a friend of Mike's.'

He ended the argument by stepping quickly through and shutting the door behind him. He turned down some stairs and reached a stone basement passage in which a faint bead of gas glimmered. He heard a murmur of voices and saw light coming from under a door.

He waited outside the door for a moment or two, with his heart beating quickly. Then he knocked loudly. The talking stopped and in a moment the door opened. He was confronted by Happy Jack himself.

'Well,' said Happy, in a slow thick voice, rather drunk, 'who are you? What do you want?'

'I'm a friend of Mike's,' said Dave. 'I've been here before. Dave Barker.'

Happy breathed heavily for some time, and looked at him as if he had not understood. He shook his head and said:

'Wash you say?'

'I'm a friend of Mike McCann,' said Dave. 'Your doorkeeper. Mike knows me well.'

'Friend o' *Mike's?*' Happy shook his head slowly.

'My name's Dave Barker.'

Happy looked at him for an unbelievably long time in silence. Dave said nothing. He was too used to rebuffs to make any effort. Then, half turning his head, Happy called:

'Mike—there'sh a chap 'ere. . . .'

In another moment Dave was pulled inside the room. He blinked round, finding himself among bright lights and strangers. Mike held him by the shoulders and started pumping his hand. Dave dropped at once into a wooden chair, leaning his elbow on a table. He was in front of another blazing fire. He gave himself up wholly to the warmth. He had found Mike, and his doss for the night.

It was a cave rather than a room he was in. It was a great vaulted cellar, with bare stone walls which arched away in the darkness far beyond the range of the gas light and fire.

The fire was a big kitchen range, glowing brightly. Above it was a rack with frying pans, and from the rack a clothes line ran, with one or two things on it : the other end was fastened somewhere in the darkness. The floor was cement—but in front of the range was a derelict and colourless square of carpet : and a bare topped table. Happy and one or two other men sat near to the table in wooden chairs, their legs stretched out towards the fire. The red light of the fire on the worn carpet looked cheerful and comfortable in the surrounding gloom.

On each side of the range built against the wall like the berths of a ship were fixed five or six sleeping bunks : each was provided with a mattress and a couple of grey blankets. On a lower bunk next to the range Mike always slept himself. Mike sat on his bunk next the fire, smoking. All round him, covering the walls and sides of his bunk, were pinned and pasted photographs of girls and men, and odd bits of letters and reminders of other scenes from his life. One of them was a newspaper cutting describing his arrest and removal to gaol after a knife fight in another town. Mike's bunk was the network of crossed and rewritten memories that most men carry only in their minds. Mike liked posing in public.

Mike and Happy were very careful about the men they let in. Only men well known to them ever found their way to the beds round the fire in this cavern. Through it passed an ever-changing flow of one and two night visitors, some coming regularly four or five times a year. To get in at all was to gain some trust and friendship from the others already there. In this way a great deal of information came to Happy's ears, and all kinds of deals, honest and dishonest, passed through his hands. He was a good fence: unlike many he acted on the square with his own clients, and gave a good hand-out. In the course of years the doss upstairs had become little more than a useful cover for comings and goings of greater purpose.

'Well, Dave, mate,' said Mike after a while, 'how are you blowing?'

'Bloody awful,' said Dave.

'Where are you going?'

'Back up home.'

'Nothing doing in London?'

'Nothing doing anywhere,' said Dave. 'Bloody awful. I dunno.'

'What you been up to, Dave?'

'Oh, nothing; nothing. An odd bit of scaffolding I got once or twice. Thankful to get twopence from anywhere for a cup of tea—Christ.'

'What are you doing now then, Dave? Going back home? When was it you were here before?'

'A year and a half ago. Things were hopeless at home. So I thought I'd see if I could get a job near London. I promised my wife I'd send for her in a year. I haven't seen her for eighteen months.'

'Is she still living at Stavely?'

'She's been there all the time. She's been ill. Now I'm going back, I've nothing to bring her.'

'You'll get your out-of-work money.'

'I used to earn four pounds and four-ten a week when we was first married,' said Dave. 'Ten years ago now. We had a decent little house, when I was working up at Handley's yard. They haven't built a boat there for eight years now: they never will.'

Dave sighed.

'Well, Mike,' he said, 'when we was kids together, who'd 'a thought it was coming to this. Glad I didn't know then. Thank Christ I'm dry for once, anyway.'

There was a clink of glass, and Happy poured out of a whisky bottle into a thick tumbler.

''Ere,' he said, 'you need a drink. Take that. Don't put no water to it.' Happy pushed half a glassful of neat whisky into his hands.

Dave clasped his hands round it and stared into the amber liquid. The aroma of whisky came into his face. He didn't like neat whisky; but it was a godsend. He took a gulp and felt it trickling like golden fire into his chest and heart, and the pit of his stomach.

'That's good,' he muttered to himself. 'Well, cheero, Mike,' he said, 'it's good to see you again.'

There was an old pear tree that grew outside the town where he used to live when he was a kid; a pear tree in an old country garden. The town had grown up all round it. It was brilliant with white blossom. It overhung the wall, and the blossom fell like snow on the roadway. Mike and he, at twelve years old, watched the little pears ripen. By August they were large and green.

In September Mike said: 'We'll pick 'em any day now.'

'We can't take 'em,' said Dave. 'It would be stealing.'

'Don't be soft,' said Mike. 'Those as overhangs the roadway is ours by right.'

It was a blazing day: hot and dusty. By now the pears were fat and yellow all over.

'You're taller than me,' said Mike. 'Hook the branch down.'

'They aren't ours,' said Dave. 'It's thieving really.'

But he pulled the bough down, and Michael picked a dozen or more enormous ones.

What a hot day that had been. The very dust in the road was a hot powder; their eyes ached from the blue of the sky. The delicious juice of the bitten pears had trickled into their dusty throats. Then an old man from inside the garden had seen them.

He waved a stick and shouted. They ran away; but Michael had stopped and thrown a stone and some bad language. Dave had it all on his mind for weeks afterwards.

God, what was the use of it all? That was twenty-five years ago. To think what he'd come to. Down and out; unable to earn a bob; without an ounce of guts left.

He looked round the cellar: looked at the other men who were staring at him; and he wondered what the hell he was doing there.

'Well,' he said to Mike in an undertone, 'I'll be glad to see my wife again. Though God knows what she'll want to see *me* for.'

'I heard she'd been ill,' said Mike. 'Haven't you got any cash at all?'

'I've got one bob,' he said, 'which I owe to Happy for a doss here to-night.'

'That's all right, Dave,' said Mike. 'We'll fix that.'

'I'll pay,' said Dave.

'Shorl right,' said Happy thickly, turning his enormous heavy face towards Dave.

Dave began feeling in his pocket for the shilling. 'Hullo,' he said, 'what in hell's this?' He brought out, entangled in his fingers, staring at it incredulously as he did so, a dainty wrist-watch and bracelet.

All the men in the room began staring at it intently, and at Dave too.

'By God, I remember,' he said. 'I picked this

thing up in the tram an hour ago, and shoved it in my pocket. I thought it was a kid's toy. I meant to give it to the conductor ; and then I dropped off to sleep and forgot it.'

'Pretty good child's toy,' said Mike. 'Here, Charley, have a look at this.'

He took the wrist watch from Dave. One of the other men came forward from the shadow and picked up the watch and examined it.

'Platinum and diamonds,' he said. 'The whole bracelet's set with brilliants—there are one or two good stones as well.'

Charley looked from the watch to Dave, and back again to the watch, without saying a word to him. He opened the back of the watch and peered inside. 'It's inscribed,' he said. 'In here. Lady something—but I'll soon take that out.'

Charley looked at Dave again. 'Your lucky day,' he said. 'Pretty good. And he told us it was a child's toy he'd picked up in the tram.'

'Drink up that drink,' said Happy. 'And you mind what you say, Charley. If he says he found it in a tram—well—'

Happy Jack, whose face was far too ponderous and heavy to smile, laughed in a wheezy, heavy voice, as if someone were playing an accordion. A faint flutter of movement passed over his drooping dewlaps.

Dave drank up his whisky. It glowed inside him now. He stretched out his legs to the fire. The heat was soaking through his rain-sodden limbs from inside and out. He began smiling to himself. The gas light and leaping fire shone brightly in his eyes, and the room was lost in shadows all round.

Mike and Happy each took some whisky and half-filled his tumbler again. He drank it in small sips.

'Well now,' said Michael. 'Cheero, Dave, me cock. Cheero. This is the first mortal drop of drink I've had to-day.'

He took a good gulp of neat whisky and said 'Ah!' And then, 'Well, Dave, looks as if you was going to take back a little present for your old woman after all.'

'What do you mean?' said Dave. 'Is there a reward on it?'

Again a suety wheeze broke from Happy.

'Thash a good 'un,' he said and drank a large gulp of whisky.

Even the pale-faced Charley smiled.

'The description of that watch is out,' he said, 'and there's a reward of three pounds offered.'

'I'll take it to the police to-morrow,' said Dave and get the three quid.'

Michael said: 'Now, Dave, you take it from us. You don't want to get mixed up with anything like that. Charley here'll get you more like fifty pounds —what do you say, Charley?'

Charley swung the watch round on his forefinger, as if it were worth nothing at all, then flipped it in the air and caught it adroitly.

'That cost a lot when it came from Bond Street,' he said. 'I'll get forty or fifty quid out of it.'

'But . . .,' said Dave.

'There you are,' said Mike. 'Don't you see, Dave—ten pounds for Charley, because he knows the game: a fiver for old Happy, because it's his business introduction, and the rule of the house—and you'll still have twenty or thirty pounds left to take home to your wife.'

Dave looked thoughtful.

'I dunno,' he said. 'I don't quite like it.'

'Wash 'e grumbling at?' said Happy. 'Not enough dough?'

'Come on, Dave,' said Mike. 'It's as good as done.'

'I've always been on the straight . . .' said Dave.

'See where it's got you,' said Charley.

There was a long pause. Mike sat with his elbows on the table, staring at Dave.

'Don't fush about that,' said Happy. 'You take the money.'

'You don't get the watch back, anyhow,' said Charley. 'I've got that. So long, all.'

He disappeared in the shadows at one end of the vault. Dave heard a door open and close—a different door from the one by which he had come in.

'There you are,' said Mike. 'That's all you have to do with it. You find a watch in a tram—you think it's only a kid's toy. Later on, you lose it. That might happen to anyone. Then a few days later you turn up here again and Happy gives you a little money in connection with a business deal.'

Happy nodded. Dave took a deep drink at his whisky. He had finished his second glass now. His limbs and head were throbbing with golden life and warmth. Mike's face, screwed up and looking at him humorously, was bobbing about talking easily. Far off floated Happy's huge jowl and mouth. Well, what they meant to do they'd have to get on with.

'Oh well,' he said, 'when do I smell the money?'

'Good boy,' said Happy. 'Thash how to talk.'

'In a week or two,' said Mike. 'You can't hardly expect it right away. You'll have to give Charley a week or so . . . How far off home are you now?'

'Two or three days' walk.'

'Well, you go home—and then come back in a fortnight's time. We'll have it for you.'

Dave wished he could have collected the reward from the police station the next day. But in the warmth of the fire all plans seemed pretty good.

'Right,' he said. 'Got anything to eat?'

'Shertainly,' said Happy. 'You ask for what you want. Now your credit's good, you'd better have a bottle of whisky. You treat yourself.'

Happy opened a new whisky bottle and put it on the table. Dave took some and passed it round.

'I'll cook you something,' said Mike.

In another ten minutes Dave was sitting before a sizzling steak. It was thick and soft: crisply brown all over, but red and juicy inside. Dave ate it slowly, hardly believing it.

'This is good,' he said after a while. 'I haven't eaten a meal like this for a year. By God, it makes you feel different.'

'Why don't you take a stroll our way now and again?' said Mike. 'Happy would put you in the way of a lot. Regular meals are worth getting.'

Dave finished his steak and stared at the fire.

'The trouble with this boy, Dave,' said Happy, 'is that he's what I'd call too nasherally honest. There's a fault in that. Any man can be too honest, just as he can be too fond of going along with women.'

They all looked at Dave, and he had nothing to say. He drank some more whisky. He stretched out his legs to the roasting fire.

'Now here's a chap in the paper this morning,' said Happy. 'I've got it here. "Local Bank Clerk Decamps With £1,800!" See that, Mike? Now there's a chap got some sense, I say. He sees a lucky moment—and takes it. And you make a fuss about this little watch.'

Dave looked round, and the room was swimming and dancing. He wondered how the bank clerk could have done such a thing. He was dog tired, and he'd drunk half a pint of neat whisky, the first alcohol he'd had for months.

'I've always been on the straight,' he heard himself saying.

'More damn fool you,' said Mike. 'Look at you, Dave. Strong, hefty fellow like you—walking about the country dead beat. Look at your muscles, Dave—you were a strong man when you were twenty-four or five. You used to take a pride in yourself. Look at your legs and arms now. You ought to be kicking yourself.'

These words bombarded Dave. It was unfair, he thought. He only wanted to sleep. They were all drinking too much whisky and getting argumentative.

'What are you getting at me for?' he said. 'We were always good friends.'

'That's why I'm talking to you,' said Mike. 'For your own good, when I see you coming in here dead beat like this. You used to take a little pride in yourself once; you could have smashed any chap in our street then, and you married the finest girl . . . I can't stand to see you coming in here looking like a damned kicked dog that can't bite back.'

'I can bite back.'

'Well, get back at the world a bit,' said Mike. 'For God's sake. What the sweet hell has it ever done for you? Downed and outed you all round. You've offered it your best, Dave, and it's treated you filth every time. Think of your last five years. If I was you, I'd get up now and show myself and my friends I wasn't such a bloody kicked dog.'

The misery of years and old despairs came rushing upon Dave in a single choking rage.

'What'd you do?'

'By Christ,' said Mike, 'I'd walk out into the town: and the first likely looking man I met in a lonely place I'd stick him up with a gun and take his money from him. That's what I'd do.'

'Then I'll do that,' said a voice out of Dave's mouth. 'I'll do it.'

'You won't,' said Mike. 'I'll bet you a fiver you won't.'

A burning, raging heat came up and filled Dave's head and the back of his eyes with fire. He jumped up and shook his clenched fist at Mike.

'I'll do it!' he shouted.

He sat back, shaking with rage—and images of the past raced by. He saw himself at twenty and twenty-one: he saw his wife when she was young, and the summer nights when they were first married. To think it had all come to this.

There was talk going on round him. Happy and Mike were talking in quiet, low voices. The fire leaped and flashed, and the room rolled round and split up in lights and shadows. 'I'll show them,' he kept on saying to himself. 'I'll show the lot of them. Why should I give up everything and be kicked, when I can stick up for myself? I'll show them I've still got some guts.'

Mike was standing up now, and he was standing up with him. Happy had put out the gas, and the other men had gone.

'Come on Dave,' said Mike. 'Let's start.'

'Start?' said Dave, and he felt his heart suddenly slogging.

'You can't go back on it now,' said Mike.

Behind his drunken anger a cold voice called

him to stop : told him he could never do it, not even once : not even for a bet. The police . . .

'We're starting now,' said Mike. 'Sober up.' Mike took his arm. The room swung round. The grate which he had been staring at for two hours was gone. His feet were feeling for stone steps leading up. He was out in the street now.

He leant against the wall for support. The pavement went racing up hill on each side of him. The rain was still coming down, and beat gentle and cold on his face. A street lamp danced and bobbed : it was a soft spot of light in the foreground, and in the far distance at the same moment. For the rest all was pitch black, save for flecks of light in the wet, shining road.

Michael was with him. He had forgotten that. Michael caught hold of his arm and drove his fingers into the muscles. It was an old trick of Mike's. The pain in his arm came through sharply.

'Pull yourself together, Dave. Walk straight, you sod. Sober up.'

'What's it all about? I'm not drunk.'

They went on slowly. Occasionally Dave lurched, and Mike clutched his arm and drove his fingers into the muscle and cursed him.

Dave tried to speak, but gave it up. The darkness flitted by them. They turned to the right, to the left, a dozen times. Through little courts and passages and small arches. The houses came at them from all angles, tilting and sliding as they came : then settled down into a steady wheeling ring. When he shook his head they broke up and went away in fragments.

They stopped for a moment near a pitch black recess. Mike caught his arm and pulled him in. Presently they heard footsteps. Mike must have heard them coming minutes before. They crouched together. The footsteps passed on the far side. They seemed to Dave an age in passing. But for the footsteps there was utter silence and blackness.

'Through here,' said Mike. And Dave stumbled through a wooden door. Dark shapes came bearing down on them, as big as houses. After a while Dave saw they were in a coal yard, with heaps of coal round them. He lurched and stumbled over loose slag. Mike clutched his arm, and the sharp pain came through.

'We've cut him off,' said Mike.

And suddenly the whole scene was vivid and clear.

They were on a canal bank : under the arch of a bridge. There was a high wall running along the bank. Behind it was the coal yard out of which they had come through a door.

A quarter of a mile away along the bank a single lamp shone. Another lamp was bracketed under the arch of the bridge overhanging the water. It cast a quiet yellow light on the muddy gravel of the towpath and the sides of the arch above. The black water shining beneath the bridge was dead and unmoving. It looked solid and thick under the yellow light. A steady drip of rain fell from the bridge on to the water. Sometimes it went out of rhythm, and a little rush of drops would leave the silence more intense.

Dave stared at the scene as if he were looking at a painted picture. It was too still and small to be really there, and the details were too clear. He felt as if he were watching the scene from outside.

Then the footsteps began again in the far distance on the muddy gravel of the path—and under the far lamp the figure of a man appeared and was lost in the darkness again. He was coming towards them. Dave found himself holding something that Mike had given him. It was a revolver. Mike clutched his arm.

'It's not loaded,' said Mike. 'It can't go off. Get back in this shadow. I'm going to get behind this buttress. But I shall be here.'

Dave nodded and stared at the revolver.

'Now Dave,' said Mike, 'it's going to be dead easy. That's a chap coming home from some office or shop. Take him suddenly. Jump out quickly and put the fear of God into him : get his arms up above his head before he knows what's happening. Got that?'

'You do it,' said Dave.

'What the hell should I do it for?' said Mike. It's what you came for. It can't go wrong. If it does, get back through this door into the coal yard. And I'll lock it after us. Can you do it?'

'Yes.'

'Right. Go through his pockets. Then make

him turn round and slip through the door and vanish.'

Dave saw it was a good plan. Trust Mike to know the ropes. After all, it was only for a bet. A bet about his having lost his guts. Suddenly he found Mike had vanished completely, and he was alone. It was damn silly, he thought, like acting. All he wanted was to get it over and get back to Happy's and sleep for twelve hours by that fire.

Suddenly the man appeared in the circle of light under the bridge. At once Dave jumped out and growled at him. He saw a look of surprise and then terror on the man's face. He was carrying an attaché case and was dressed in a macintosh and a bowler hat. He dropped the case and put up his arms. Only once did he try to grab Dave's arm. A voice came from the shadows.

'Stop that. There's another gun covering you.'

After that it was absurdly quick and easy. Dave went through his pockets and took out a wallet. He wrenched open the bag, which was locked. He took out a bundle of papers, and saw there were a few pound notes. He put everything into his own jacket. A moment later he and Mike were both in the coal yard again, and the door was locked behind them. They hurried across. 'Did it really happen?' Dave kept asking himself. 'I can't remember it clearly at all. I can't remember what happened.'

'That was damn good, Dave,' said Mike. They reached the end of the yard and the shed beyond. 'We'd better go separately. I'll take the back yards. You keep to the roads. I'll tell you the way.'

Dave's dream went on. He dragged his legs mechanically: shadows and roads went by. Then he came to the door of Happy's. The big grate was still burning downstairs; its red glow was the only light. He fell into a bunk, kicking off his boots and rolling up his coat to make a pillow. Instantly a delicious tide of sleep, black and visionless, flowed over him. . . .

Dave woke up feeling a new man. He swung his legs out of his bunk and stretched. He looked round. The underground vault was almost in darkness, but a single shaft of bright sunlight, thick with dancing motes, came through a grating high up in the wall. It must be broad daylight outside.

The sun picked out a small patch of light. It fell on Mike sitting at the table in a shirt and trousers, eating bacon and drinking tea from a tin mug. Dave walked from his bunk to the light. When Mike saw him he jumped up and shouted:

'Come on! How are you blowing, Dave?'

Dave sat down by the table and scratched his head. 'I feel a bit muddled.'

'You want some breakfast,' said Mike. 'A couple of good back rashers'll do you a lot of good. You'll find a pump in the upstairs room. Go and have a clean.'

Dave went up and washed his chest and arms in ice-cold water, and came back shaking water from his hair. When he came back he found Happy was talking to Mike, while Mike fried more bacon by the fire.

'Well youngshter,' said Happy. 'Slept like a baby, didn't yer? Now show us what you've brought back."

As he said it, Dave felt a sudden rush of blood and fear in his heart. It had all happened, then.

He walked slowly over to his bunk and brought back his jacket. Happy took it from him and took out the wallet and the bulky bundle of papers. Dave saw some pound notes among them, just as he had put them in his pocket the night before. Happy pulled a bundle of pound notes out of the wallet.

'Thatsh a fifty,' he said, 'and thash two folded up fives. Not a bad shtart.'

He began arranging the other bundles of papers over the table. As he did so, Dave saw that there were more notes : and more still : packets of them. Then he saw that the whole bundle of papers which he had brought was made up of packets of pound notes. Some in envelopes and wrappers, still with the bank's name on them.

'There's seven or eight hundred there,' said Happy.

'Count them,' said Mike. 'Don't play with them.'

Happy rubbed his hands together. Then he seized Mike by the shoulders and danced, shaking his sixteen stone like a basin of jelly. His mournful face jerked about with its drooping folds as sad as ever. Then he sat down and wheezed and began to count.

'Look here, Mike,' said Dave, 'count me out of this. You tricked me into it; I was drunk, and you tricked me into it. There didn't seem anything in it to go sticking up the first chap who came by for a bet. But look at all this. I'm not going to get mixed up with robbing someone of all this. I'm serious.'

'All right, Dave,' said Mike. 'You did your part damn well. Don't get cold feet now.'

'But the police'll be after this business like a knife.'

'Don't you worry, Mashter Dave,' said Happy. 'There ain't going to be no policeman after this lot. They're looking for a bank clerk what took away £1,800. He's the fellow they're after. And he's not likely to go telling them someon'sh took half of it off him. No fear.'

Dave worked his fingers together and frowned.

'Don't you see, Dave?' said Mike. 'That chap was the bank clerk we were reading about in the paper. "Local Bank Clerk Decamps With £1,800." It's as safe as sitting in your own arm chair. He won't tell what's happened. Nobody knows but him. He's got half of it left, and he'll be out of the country to-morrow.'

'I'll be ——' said Dave. 'It's a million to one chance that's turned up. I go and take this on for a bet, too drunk to know what I'm doing, and pick on the very chap that's gone off with all this money, and we get half of it off him.'

Happy laughed and spat.

'It's not luck,' he said. 'It was all planned out, Dave, my boy. Don't you see that. We knew all about that bank clerk : knew just where he was—and where he was going. Why he'd been working with us for years ; and this time he was trying to double-cross us. We'd planned to get the stuff off him just at that very place—then in you walked, and Mike made you take it on for a bet.'

'Your turning up,' said Mike, 'made it all gravy. He'd have known me. Now he can't know who in hell's done it.'

Dave got up and took his coat.

'It's no good,' he said. 'Split without me.'

Mike caught his arm and drove his fingers in.

'Cut out that baby talk, Dave,' he said. 'You make me bloody sick. You're going to split that lot with me and Happy. You did the best part of the work, and you did it fine. Here, eat your breakfast, Dave.'

He put the bacon he had cooked before him, still crackling in the pan. He tore off a chunk of the loaf with his hands, and poured strong tea into a tin mug.

All the time Dave ate they talked to him.

'What the hell's the good of not taking your split?' said Mike. 'Happy and I'll split it alone, that's all. The bank won't get it back, anyway. You earned that money, Dave. You got a bit of luck—for God's sake take it. Have some guts. Think of that wife of yours, and what you could do with it.'

'It'd be downright wicked of you not to take it,' said Happy. 'Man like you, with a wife.'

'Think of all the bloody luck you've had,' said Mike. 'Now a bit of good luck comes your way, you take it. Why, you could buy a decent little cottage, or fit up a shop.'

Later, Mike and Dave went out to a pub. After Dave had got a couple of pints inside him, he gave up arguing. It was a fine thing to have ten bob in your pocket, to be able to stand a pint of beer. He began to think of getting home to his wife and breaking the news. He saw himself meeting her after eighteen months: then telling her, and showing her the money.

They made the split that afternoon in Happy's cellar.

'You can't take your lot away at once,' said Happy. 'It all needs handling. Thash where I come in. But you take one or two quid away now, that'll be safe enough.'

'How many chaps come in to your place every night?' asked Dave.

'About fifteen or twenty,' said Happy, 'upstairs; there are about six or ten of us down here. Shay thirty all told.'

'Let's make our split,' said Dave, 'and leave something over. Then give everyone who comes in here to-night ten bob—and a damn good spread with plenty of booze.' Think what it would mean to most of them on the tramp like I've been.'

Happy and Mike looked at each other. Happy stroked his huge jowl for a long time. Then he began to choke and laugh.

'We'll give 'em champagne,' he said. 'Thash the idea.'

He went on wheezing and choking in chords of laughter like a broken and punctured accordion played by a drunk man.

At about eight o'clock that evening Mike stood in front of the stove in the upstairs room of Happy's doss, ready to ladle out food to all comers. He had put on a white apron and a white chef's cap for the party. He was a small, alert fellow, with a wrinkled, humorous face : he was fond of posing and showing off in public. Soon everyone was calling him 'chef'.

Happy had disappeared and slept all the afternoon. Mike and Dave had arranged it all. They had run a couple of the trestle and board tables down the middle of the room, and had covered them in new, shining American cloth with a red and white check pattern. There were no lights in the place save a couple of dim bracket lamps which were never used : it was the leaping red glow of the big fire which brought everyone to Happy's. And that was all anyone usually needed.

But to-night Dave and Mike had got in a couple of dozen candles and massed them down the table in a sparkling guttering row, stuck in the necks of empty whisky and beer bottles. Apart from the table, the whole place was in its usual dimness.

Mike had roasted in the range below an immense joint of ribs of beef. Pounds of potatoes and carrots had been boiled together in a great two-handled billy can. On the top of the stove the beef and vegetables stood smoking. The table glistened with candles and brand new white enamel plates. A small barrel of beer stood ready tapped at one end of the table.

Then Happy came in, dragging a big basket; and he placed with great care at regular intervals on the American cloth half a dozen bottles of Cordon Rouge.

As each new arrival came into Happy's that night, he stopped and stared; and asked himself where the hell he was getting to. Lights; a spread table; a man in a chef's cap; champagne. That was what he saw. Dave or Mike took each man of them by the arms as he came in and brought him over to the fire to shake hands with Happy. Happy laughed and wheezed and drank by the fire.

'It'sh a little party,' he said to the newcomers. 'A blow-out that'll make your belly bust, all free and nothing to pay. It'sh a friend of mine, Dave Barker, as is shtanding it. 'E's 'ad a bit of luck with an inveshtment.'

At a little after eight they began to eat. At first the men coming in were too dead beat to warm up to it. They came up to the table silent and weary, and sat with their torn sleeves resting on it, staring and amazed. There were one or two burly men who by natural gift and long practice could make a good enough thing out of the road; but most of them were tired to death, with stubbly beards and pale, sunken faces. Soon the good beef began to gladden them, and the heat of the room and the copious pints of free beer to make their hearts beat faster; and a roar of conversation began. The men who could make jokes began shouting them out. Mike, standing by the joint, was ready with answers. Most of the jokes were sarcastic comments about the table arrangements and food, based on a mock refinement and luxury to which the men pretended they were used. It was a bitterness turned to wit; an irony on their own lives, taking its bite from the intensity of their want and the brutality in which they really lived. It was the wit of the gaols, a wit that is muttered under the breath with unmoving lips in exercise yards: the most apt, the most allusive, the most secret wit in the world. But at Dave Barker's party it broke out into loud shouts.

The excitement rose when Happy opened the champagne. Most of the men had never drunk champagne before. Others made pretence of disgust at their loud hiccups and choking. Then Happy spoke from the end of the table, and in Dave Barker's name made every guest a present of ten shillings. The noise rose to a tumult of shouting. At first half of the men thought that it was a new joke —a piece of ironic wit in their own vein, as if one of them meeting a friend had said: 'Well, how's tricks, mate?' and the answer had been: 'Not so bad—a fellow came up to me an hour ago and gave me half a quid—'

But immediately they found it was true indeed, and Mike and Dave went round the table and laid in front of each man the money itself—in silver and coppers. They put the money away quickly and fearfully—and presently they began shouting for Dave to make a speech.

Mike waved his big iron ladle from his post near the food and dragged Dave forward.

Dave was no speech maker: but he was fairly drunk by now, and he had been living in an unreal dream world for the past twelve hours and more. He found twenty or thirty strange faces staring at him. The men gave him a ragged cheer. He saw only the candles, the faces turned towards him.

Dave began to tell them about the first thing that came into his own mind—himself: his own life. As he spoke, his strange dream seemed to open out and doors were thrown wide in his mind. The white pear blossom came drifting across, snow against the azure sky: and he saw his wife, with the black lustrous hair and the white throat of her youth. Then he saw the wheeling shadow of the hard times swing across his town and settle on men's homes like a blight. The hungry thousands with sunken eyes and faces pressed round and called to him—from cheap dosses and cheerless wards and crypts that took in the destitute, from the open, from doorsteps and prison cells where they had been scattered. And he felt his own life merge into the lives of the many thousands of men like him : once whole, and now broken.

As he spoke, Dave Barker ceased to wonder how he came to be doing it at all ; and he gave utterance to feelings that flowed round him from many places.

He began talking about the police—defending himself against them.

'Once you're down,' he said, 'the police are bound to be against you. People who've got something can't ever see it like that. The police are put there to *protect* people's property. But if you've got no property, the police can't protect you. A chap like me—like some of you—who's been stripped ; had no job, no money, no dry clothes and can't get any : who has tried for years and is still right down, he's a danger to people who have got something. Who knows when he's not going to break out? And by God he doesn't know himself. You must break out sometimes. Once you're down, the police are against you. Anybody who's been down knows that. . . .'

He paused. A strange and unexpected silence fell over the whole group of men. Dave Barker looked up. He saw Happy was standing at the foot of the table, talking to two men. One was a police sergeant : the other a plain clothes officer. They had come in unnoticed in the noise.

The whole room fell quiet. The two police officers stared round. They saw the thirty men sprawled round Happy's table. They saw empty champagne bottles rolling over the table. They saw thirty candles glittering : empty plates pushed back here and there. One or two men had left the table and were lying on mattresses round the stoves, smoking. Over all hung a gathering fog of pungent tobacco smoke.

Dave came towards the police officers. His heart beat suddenly, and he cursed himself and Mike and Happy.

'Well,' the police sergeant said to Happy, 'what's the meaning of all this?'

'Meaning of what?' said Happy slowly.

The policeman nodded at the room.

Happy waited, looking at them. He wheezed heavily, and frowned. He said nothing for a long time, looking as if he did not know what they were asking him to explain.

'Did you want to shee me, Sir?' he said at length.

'What's it all about?' said the Inspector again.

'It's just a little party,' said Happy.

'Party,' said the Inspector. 'You'd better tell us, Happy. Where's all the champagne come from.'

Happy stared dully round the table.

'Champagne?' he said, and gave a laugh of deprecation. 'That'sh only a little fun, sir. Just a few empty bottlesh, to make a little joke. We can't afford *real* champagne here! This is only a cheap doss house, you know, for poor men. It'sh a poor man's place.'

The officers strode up to the table and looked round. The loose money had all vanished.

Happy looked at the officers with great respect and went on: 'Did you come for anything? Always pleased to help if there'sh anything I can do.'

The two police officers strode round the room. They stared at Dave Barker—and the other men. Happy followed them closely.

'What I came for, Mr. Happy, is this,' said the sergeant. 'We're on the look out for a very valuable wrist watch that's been lost. Left in a tram, the lady thinks. You keep your eye open for it—and if you see a chap in here with it, don't let him get away with it.'

'A wrist watch,' said Happy. 'Why, there was a chap brought a wrist watch in 'ere only to-night. He didn't know where to take it, so he gave it to me—and I wash going to bring it round to the station to-morrow morning.'

'We'll take it now,' said the sergeant.

'Ah,' said Happy, laughing throatily. He signalled to Charley behind his back.

'You didn't think there was no chance of it not coming?' he said. 'Why I told you it'd been brought in 'ere. It'sh a lucky thing this is an honest place. Otherwise that watch might have gone astray. It'sh a poor doss house, this: but it's honest. Was that what you came round about?'

'You hand that watch over now,' said the sergeant.

While he was speaking, Happy had taken the watch from Charley.

'Of course, of course,' he said. 'Here'sh the watch. Didn't you say there wash a three pounds reward?'

'Yes,' said the sergeant. 'Call at the police station to-morrow.'

The police officers still showed signs of looking round curiously. Happy bowed them politely towards the door, wheezing and coughing.

'Good-bye, Sir,' he said. 'Good-bye. What a lucky thing it wash me that watch got brought to. I'm always ready to help you offishers.'

The two police officers glared at him. They felt he was too tipsy to be worth talking to any further. Besides he had given them the watch so promptly; and they had no suspicions about his larger operations.

After they had gone, Dave went up to Happy.

'Bloody hell,' he said. 'I've had enough of this. I thought they'd got on to that other thing.'

'Don't you think about it,' said Happy. 'It simply ain't possible. They got that watch off me. That's all they'd come for. They won't worry about thish place now. That'll have done me quite a lot of good. You go round and get that three pound reward, Dave, to-morrow; if you got the guts.'

But Dave did not collect the reward the next

day, whether it was lack of guts or some other quality that kept him away. Dave went home by train, in a new blue serge suit. His heart was light and hopeful. He'd walked to London, and come back home in a train. The whole thing was a hand out from fate, and it was useless to fight against it.

It was Happy himself who collected the three pounds reward. The police gave him the reward, and decided that Happy's doss was a harmless, innocent sort of place. They did not see, nor did the lady who owned the watch ever discover, that Charley the jeweller had removed all the sapphires from the inside, and exchanged the two large diamonds in the bracelet for high quality paste. He did it really artistically. So Charley cleared seventy quid on it, too.

THE THREE PRIESTS

Once inside the church, the breath of decay was pungent. It was dark and silent, the air undisturbed throughout the week.

Across the door hung a red and black baize curtain. It smelt damp and rotten against the face. The iron railing on which it hung was scaling away in brown rust flakes. A heavy fustiness came from the stack of old hymnals; their black cloth covers were falling away with age and mould, their printed leaves breathing out a rotten dampness. In the gloom small spots of mildew shone green and phosphorescent on the straw-stuffed cushions of the pews. The smell of ancient woodwork, damp rot, dry rot, mingled everywhere. The crumbling mortar of the walls, the grey stone flags under which men were buried, gave out their own breaths. A dozen stale and heavy odours were brewed together undisturbed, unchanged, unfreshened from one week's end to another.

In the dusk of the autumn evening one uncertain oil lamp hung and swung on a chain above the choir. It moved gently, casting its forlorn lights and shadows in slowly weaving circles on the nave, the empty pews, the lectern, and the carved screen. The corners of the church behind the massive stone pillars were lost in darkness. Against the windows, which still gleamed faintly grey with the day's last light, overgrown ivy branches rustled and tapped, as if trying to get in. In the belfry were startings and creaks of woodwork and movements and voices of birds.

Alone in the church, standing under the swinging lamp in the half gloom and changing light an old man conducted the service of evensong. Alone and unanswered he read the canticles and psalms; crossed to the lectern; gave out the lessons to the empty church: read the priest's part of the responses. He gave pauses as he read, for the congregation to follow him.

Arthur Underwood was seventy-five. His voice shook, and was taken up with faint echoes in the silence. His hands quavered at the lectern. His dim eyes and failing memory mistook the pages, gave out the wrong lesson, made foolish mistakes in the familiar office. He paused and felt ashamed, and corrected his mistakes. But there was not a soul to see or to criticize or to wonder at his mumbling: no one to reproach him but himself.

He found himself in the pulpit. What was he thinking of? How could he preach to an empty church? If only there had been a handful of people: if only there had been one person, one child, to whom he could have said good-bye. Or if only he could have had a word with Allistair, his neighbour in the next parish: but Allistair was too far above him; a recluse, an ascetic; a saint for all he knew.

This was Underwood's last service; the last time he would ever stand in his pulpit or before his lectern: the last time he would lock up after

Sunday evensong, hang up his surplice in the vestry and take the cobbled path through the dark churchyard ; through the broken garden ; into the vicarage ; through the stone paved kitchen and the firelight and warmth.

He stood in the pulpit and passed a trembling hand across his face. Forty years. But where were the last ten ? Dark bat-winged dreams at the nightmare hour.

Past them he saw his life clearly as it had been thirty years ago : before the War. Then he had worked in the July sun with the men : drunk beer with them, crouching in the blue-black shadows of noon. The village had been full of good men then, and his church populous with the men and their families. One Sunday the bishop came ; the old bishop, who had been his friend, who had given him the Clere Crucis living. It was a hot morning, and the church was full for matins. The door stood wide open all through the service, and the sunlight came pouring in on the flags : with it the murmur of bees rising and falling, and the delicious breath of the lime trees. After matins in the hot sunlight the people waited for half an hour talking in the churchyard and the lane, and he walked from one group to another.

He looked round at the empty church and the bright vision disappeared. The good men were all gone. They had left him alone. Now old age and rheumatism shut him in, locking his chin upon his breast, twisting his hands into trembling, contorted shapes. He stood in the pulpit, and the years sank down on him like shapes in a dark and terrifying dream. He clasped his hands before his face and sank on to the stone floor of the pulpit in an agony of weeping. He flung his arms across the reading desk of the pulpit and prayed.

Above him the lamp turned with circles of sad light. The dark shadows wheeling and weaving, the fluttering light choked by the shadows. With it a hundred vague shapes of failure and despair turned round him. Could these pictures be real? The empty, desolate church, the acrid smell of decay in his nostrils, the utter loneliness, the taste of his own salt tears upon his mouth—could he really be that young Arthur of forty and fifty years ago? Through the old memories, darkened and confused by drink, the dim flame of his mind still upward flickering, prayed for consolation and forgiveness, for strength to meet the last few years.

When he was calm, he left the pulpit, read out the last hymn, and gave the blessing. He hung up his surplice in the vestry and put on his coat. He lowered the oil lamp on its cord and blew it out. A moment later he was feeling, in the darkness, for the door handle with the musty curtain in his face. A cold night wind blew into the church. For a few minutes he stood with his hand on the door, gazing back into the darkness behind him.

The vicarage of Clere Crucis was surrounded by elm trees which dwarfed and darkened it. They were black and motionless in the gathering gloom of the evening. The church was behind the vicarage. The village itself lay farther down the road at a little distance. Beyond it the road climbed out on to the windy high ground leading to the hamlet of Upper Crucis on the moors.

Hugh Beresford stood at the wooden gate of the drive of Clere Crucis vicarage. He was a middle aged man with closely cut grey hair. His figure was slightly stooping and thin, his clothes worn. His face was lined and stamped with care from many years of curacies in large towns, with a family dependent upon him. He placed his hand on the gate and saw that the hinges were falling away from the rotten woodwork. Inside the gravel drive was weed grown: the grass banks and lawns wild and unkempt with fern fronds knee and waist high.

The house stood with empty windows inky black in the dusk. Hugh remembered the garden twenty years ago on summer afternoons, when tea was brought out on a silver tray and there was the sound of the mower, and a piano in the distance playing a Chopin polonaise that came and went in dreamy snatches on the summer air.

As the ghost-like sound haunted him, old memories and longing for lost years and for his boyhood were overwhelming. A Chopin polonaise half-heard across lawns and clipped hedges . . .

As he looked at the house, mournful and dispossessed of life, damp, slatternly, unpainted, it seemed incredible that Arthur Underwood, whom he knew as a boy, had been living week by week, year by year, in this tangle of vegetation and mildew. How had he lived, he wondered, how had he changed?

Hugh strolled to the stable yard at the back of the house, which he remembered alive with sunlight and with the clatter of horses. Now his foot slipped on cobbles moist and green with moss. One coach-house door swung loose and unlatched. The outhouses round the yard were unpainted and rotten with their roofs sagging and many fallen tiles : in one shed he found a heap of empty whisky bottles ; in another broken gardening tools. He turned into a sidewalk to come round to the front of the house again. The laurel shrubbery was in the wildest disorder, with tangled undergrowth waist and chest high. The smell of rank vegetation was in his nostrils, and birds flew up startled from the thickets.

He came again to the front of the house and hesitated before the front door. He looked through the coloured glass panes ; he pulled the bell and a wheezy creak of wire followed, but no answering ring. Presently he heard footsteps inside, and felt his heart suddenly beating at the thought of entering his new home.

A man opened the door : Underwood's one old servant. He must have been sixty-five or seventy, but his body was still straight and massive, and his shoulders square. He was dressed in a sailor's blue jersey over tweed trousers, and wore a tweed cloth cap on his head. His face was rugged and unyielding, and lined as if it had been rough hewn from granite.

'How do you do, Collyer,' said Hugh. 'You got my letter?'

Collyer looked at him with a surly expression, but made no answer.

'I'll come in,' said Hugh. He had to push past the man into the bare-boarded hall. There was an intense silence in the house, and a fustiness of old boards. He opened doors and looked at the tall empty rooms. This used to be the drawing room, this the dining room, this overshadowed room a study. Against the study windows rustled the leaves of the overgrown laurels, pressing like curious hands. The room was filled with dark gloomy green. He tried the window catch, but it was stuck.

'I put the bed in here,' said Collyer.

Hugh saw a small camp bed in one corner of the empty room. Beside it a rickety tin tripod held up an enamel basin : and a chipped enamel ewer stood on the bare boards.

'Couldn't you have got me up a table and chair or rug for a few days?' said Hugh.

'You only asked for a bed,' said Collyer.

'Is all Mr. Underwood's furniture moved out?'

'He didn't have much left these last few years. He sold it piece by piece to pay for bare board and lodging. That's the way your church treats its faithful old servants nowadays. I wonder you couldn't wait, rather than rush in before the print of his old feet was cold on these floors.'

This was said with such quiet steady anger that Hugh was startled. He looked at Collyer earnestly. Collyer shifted his gaze and gave no response. He reeked of whisky.

'I came at the bishop's special request,' said Hugh. 'He wanted the church to be opened on Sunday.'

'Mr. Underwood could have done the service next Sunday and for many months yet. Why did you need to go tearing him out by the roots?' Collyer gave him a fierce, sullen stare.

Hugh began to like him.

'It's no doing of mine,' he said. 'We can't argue about it. I'm sorry if Mr. Underwood was put to any difficulty.'

Collyer looked at him scornfully and folded his arms.

'Difficulty,' he said, 'he'd plenty of that: left in his old age by the church he served all his days. I'm only a simple bloody sailor, but my service looks after its men, and my pension comes in every month. B' Chris',' he said, 'we don't turn a man off when he's old and ill and his bones rotten with disease.'

They stared at each other. Collyer's anger burnt like a clear flame in the deathly silent house, with its smell of decay.

'You do the church a wrong to talk like that,' said Hugh. 'It is in every respect a finer service than the navy. As you are a friend of Mr. Underwood's, you ought to know that his pension is going to be a charge of two pounds a week on this living: that is, on my income.'

Collyer said nothing: but Hugh saw that his simple directness had made an impression.

'I shall go and look at the church,' he said. 'Did you get me anything to eat?'

'You didn't ask for anything to eat,' said Collyer. 'But there's some bread and cheese here.'

Hugh left the house and crossed the tangled front garden. With senses slightly heightened he looked towards the church—a dark outline in the gloom with groups of elms surrounding it.

It was now the very hour of dusk when the grass turns grey, the hedgerows black, and the distant barks of dogs ring on the air. In the churchyard a tense silence had fallen.

Hugh saw the grass on the graves was too long for anything but a scythe A couple of sheep had strayed in through a gap in the broken wall. As he approached he felt the church was sinking in a rising tide of decay. The long grass rose and lapped its sides. Dark green moss came to a higher level than his own eyes. The draining gutters were choked and filled with earth. Thick creepers were dragging the fabric down and crumbling the mortar from the stones. On the north side two fissures in the wall were caused by a subsidence. Above the fissures the roof was strained and sinking, and slates had already fallen.

Hugh walked silently round the church, noting the damage. Already he was beginning to see it in his mind in terms of builders' estimates; of mortgages; of money to be raised; of weeks of argument, pleading for funds, obstruction from every side: his will and strength against the forces of decay; his spirit against the deadly inertia of matter, against the endless, mindless attack of decay and retrogression, that dragged buildings down in a wilderness of roots and creepers, turning form and order back into chaos and darkness, crumbling the Christian churches in every country week by week, thought by thought, stone by stone . . .

He turned in the leaden dusk to the church door and opened it. At once the rotting door curtain blew in his face, the door slammed behind him with a crash, and he stood in the darkness, breathing the very morphew of decay.

He saw the points of green mould faintly luminous like watching eyes in the silence. He smelt the damp stone, the decay of woodwork, fabrics, leather. He heard the overgrown ivy tapping at the windows as if to force an entry. Rustles of life and flutterings of wings in the roof told him the birds were already there. Voices and whisperings of despair began to assail him. The church was a wilderness already. Arthur had let the decay break in too far.

In the vestry he lit the lamp and found an empty pipe lying on the table; it was very old, almost filled with a black carbon crust, with one side broken away: the mouthpiece was discoloured, jagged, bitten. At once he began to feel Arthur himself was there. In the empty cupboards where his vestments had hung were Arthur's thoughts and feelings: in the chests, Arthur's prayers: and Arthur's slow despair and yielding. Phrases began to run in Hugh's head, hurried, anxious phrases; the words of a letter he would write to the bishop, saying that the task was beyond him, the parish too far sunk in decay, he himself too old and tired for this new endeavour.

Later that night Hugh made an effort to look through the papers he had brought. But all the time the thought of Arthur Underwood distracted him and the figure of the old man hovered in the background of his thoughts, just beyond the circle of the lamplight.

Hugh sat on a small camp bed in the corner of the empty room, and spread his documents in the glow of the lamp on the bare-boarded floor. The last surveyor's certificate, fifteen years out of date; the new estimate, including re-drainage and re-roofing; four hundred pounds—to make the house merely sanitary and weatherproof; the builder's preliminary report on the church, his own draft of a report to the churchwardens; lists of local names for subscriptions; suggestions for printers who might supply work free; a letter from the diocesan secretary of finance concerning the parish quota. He felt his blood and strength ebbing away into an endless effort to create money and to conjure up money out of nothing.

Then there was the bishop's letter. He looked through the documents and spread it out to read again.

'Your predecessor Underwood was, as you may have heard, far advanced in age and in infirmities for which we cannot blame him. He had also of late years given way to the most deplorable intemperance, and in the grip of this failing he allowed the whole state of the church in the parish of Clere Crucis to fall into a state of grievous neglect.

'It is useless now to waste words on his shortcomings. The consequences of his neglect, however, we have to bear. I refer not only to the state of religion in this parish, but more especially to the fabric of the church itself and the repair of the vicarage house—once a really valuable property.

'I enclose a draft estimate which was recently made for the Diocesan Board in connection with the Clere Crucis vicarage and grounds, which you had better study in detail. The surveyor's certificate, which should of course be renewed every five years, has been allowed to lapse completely. In the absence of any attempt at co-operation from Underwood the Dilapidations Board have been unable to do anything.

'Turning to the parish itself, a fund is urgently needed for church repair. One of your first duties will be to inspire a *local* fund for this purpose. The parish of Clere Crucis must help itself in this respect. In fact, the contribution of Clere Crucis to the Diocesan quota has been almost non-existent for some years now.

'The cause of the church has also, I am afraid, been *unwisely* served by your neighbour, Allistair. His misdirected zeal, and leanings towards ritualism, wholly unsuited to a simple congregation, have all but emptied his church and won him great personal enmity.'

Hugh put the letter down. He had been waiting for years to meet Allistair: some said he was the finest man in the diocese. When he first went to his parish, many years ago, he had been subjected to acts of violence. There had been stone-throwing. But they had left him alone since.

He turned back to the papers. The yellow lamplight fell on the confused pages of forms, figures, accounts, estimates, indentures. Hugh read on.

'The governors of Queen Anne's bounty are the central authority under the Ecclesiastical Dilapidations measure of 1923 to 1927. Theirs is the authority under which payments are collected for future repairs ordered upon surveyors' certificates. In the case of a benefice not exceeding £300 per annum in annual value the Governors may make a grant for dilapidations according to an agreed scheme: money may be lent for improvements and dilapidations in seven or ten years terms. Payments vary at the discretion of the Diocesan Dilapidation Board.'

The ways and means of his private life began to

run through Hugh's head. Out of a nominal income of £350 he had to pay two pounds a week to Underwood's pension, renovate the vicarage, buy food and clothing for his children and educate them, pay the expenses of his wife's illness. It was fantastic. He would have to go cap in hand to Queen Anne's Bounty, plead for an education grant, postpone the doctor's bill—this was what his priesthood had come to. He stood up and swept the papers away with his foot. The burden was hopeless, crushing, absurd.

He opened the door, paced from one bare room to another. His feet rang on the boards, breaking the night silence of the empty vicarage. He saw his wife sleeping in her bed, and confused images filled his mind of the threadbare, crowded life of his little home where every minute and every space was overcrowded. Now he was suddenly utterly alone, and he could look on the days and years of his life as if they were a story.

There had been hope once, and the fervours of boyhood, and age-long silences. God is indwelling and the path is up the breast of a hill where the whole hill-side is illuminated with a flood of clear light filling the air, blue and cold like upper ice. Prayer brings the soul close to God through Christ. There is an intense silence on the hill-side, and the grasses and rose-tangled hedges are motionless in the air. There are long hours of prayer and indwelling. The trees are filled with music; something flies out of the prison bars and soars upwards into the light, until the radiance is more blinding than darkness, and the hours longer than a thousand years.

The light is lost, the road leads down into darkness, dryness, loss, banishment, the endless struggle with material difficulties: raising money out of nothing; studying investments, getting into debt; arguing, sighing, weeping; losing heart; losing your temper.

Hugh leant his forehead in the dark against the peeling wallpaper: an elderly priest with a heart full of material cares, caught in the dead, meaningless gestures of a dead church. His thoughts and feelings of twenty-five years ago lay before him, without life: old hopes and fears; fears long ago fulfilled; hopes that no longer mattered; suffering that no longer hurt, like dead and dried corpses of small forest animals, over which a child might weep.

Wind was filling the elms round the garden, and a sound like the roar of the distant sea welled up all through the house. The wainscot creaked, the key in the lock rattled, a door banged; there were movements in every wall and ceiling.

Hugh could almost see Arthur Underwood. He could hear him walk, feel him breathe and sigh and moan in the empty rooms. The house was all his: its night sounds were the sounds of his despair. Night after night, year after year, he wandered from room to room with a candle in his shaking hand. The church clock struck one and two. Hugh followed and traced out his agony and long-drawn death in life. Soon he himself would feel as Arthur had felt. His body was old, and tired of its journey, his spirit exhausted. His wife and children pressed round him asking for strength and hope in the world that he could never give them. The difficulties of his life loaded him like chains. He sank on his knees and muttered: 'Where, oh where, have I missed the way?'

Intense darkness filled his soul, the darkness of the house, the darkness of years; the darkness covering his own life: the dead darkness of a decaying church, and the horror of a world from which God has turned away . . . broken cities of past times, and seething hordes in the darkness, torturing, lusting, destroying . . .

His thoughts drove him out of the house, and he walked for hours; round him the trees and shadows weaving, threshing and whistling in the wind. The road shone white before him, rising towards high ground. He walked on, the mechanical rhythm of his own steps drugging him as he went. Gradually as the air grew grey with approaching dawn his thoughts became clearer.

It was early in the morning, and the dawn was trembling through a grey ground mist when he reached the village of Upper Crucis. He was impelled to look for his neighbour Allistair's church. He opened the door quietly and sat down at the back.

The church, shrouded at first in misty air, was

very small, scarcely larger than a saint's chapel turning off the aisle of a cathedral. It was a minute gem of early Norman : white, simple, perfectly preserved. The interior walls showed the rough shapes of unhewn stones. A beam of cold morning light began to fall in through the east window, filling the church with a pure, frozen light like iced wine. In its rays the whitewash of the walls was soft and brilliant. The pew cushions were blue. A blue silk damask hung from the lectern and the altar. The altar was decorated with a simple mass of white chrysanthemums in a tall silver ewer. The eastern sun flashed on the silver and the flowers.

As Hugh waited, the weariness of his limbs vanished. A feeling of calmness began to flow over him like a deep river, as if there were a calmness in the air of the church itself. He sighed, filling his lungs with the freshets of morning air. As the light grew clearer and whiter, a nimbus of radiance shone all round the altar. To Hugh it seemed that the blue silk of the altar cloth, the white of the flowers, the flash of the burnished silver became splendid with the very essence of their own colours ; so that he saw blue and white and silver for the first time. His body was filled with deep and trembling breaths. His heart beat with the clearness of the blue. The radiance of the white filled his lungs, and the chalice ran like silver fire in his veins and silver music in his ears. He found on the pew ledge in front of him a book of meditations, and, opening it, read the words :—

'Then will he sometimes peradventure send out a beam of ghostly light piercing this cloud of unknowing that is betwixt thee and Him, and show thee some of His secrets, the which man may not and cannot speak. Then shalt thou feel thine affection inflamed with the fire of his love, far more than I can tell thee. For of that work that pertaineth only to God dare I not take upon me to speak to thee with my blabbering fleshly tongue.'

Presently Hugh saw that Allistair had come into the church, and had begun to celebrate the communion service. He and Allistair were alone in the church. His eyes were drawn irresistibly to Allistair's. The eyes were deep set, the face sensitive, intellectual. But it was the eyes that compelled Hugh. They were windows opening into unknown depths of strength and serenity, making the face calm, light, illuminated with peace. With the clear beams of the east sun round him, the priest seemed to Hugh to be one with the luminous light and the white walls of the church. Hugh saw that he lived in the strength and life of many hundreds of years: that the life of the building, and of its priests since Norman days, of its prayers and worship, shone in this man with renewed radiance, with light and fire, fresh and glittering from the fountain-head.

Hugh closed his eyes and still the light was poured into them, and the clear air shone though. The walls receded everywhere, the doors flew open, the roof melted away to the emblazoned distances, to the scent of roses and the silver radiance of the sky.

He breathed and filled his heart with a trembling sigh; for an instant that was longer than all his life or any human life, a piercing light struck him, utterly dissolving the prison of time, of sense, of selfhood.

There is music in the sky spaces, silence in the crash of the sea over rocks. Red ants are like modern soldiers creeping with steel casques and weapons of death. Man-killing tigers lie in the sun and purr like kittens. Some martyrs feel no pain when they are tortured. Men and women in public houses talk as angels do. Colours can be heard, and music seen. The smallest fly is too big for thought, and mystics have seen the universe smaller than a hazel nut. Criminals know secrets hidden from judges and bishops. Somewhere a cock crows at midnight: a drunk man forms prayers to a broken statue.

There are a thousand million men alive in the world now: and the world is many æons old. Each man that lives or has ever lived knows God and is known to God. All else is visible and divisible. Only God can be visible and invisible, divisible and indivisible: old scraps of liturgy, thaumaturgy, magic encrusted, potent. The farthest star and the smallest water-worm a turn of his eyebrow, a breath of his nostril; every bird that cuts the air an immense world of light.

In the ocean depths, life: in the dust of the

streets, life ; in the dead, life : in the dying, living. For ever in the ebb and flow, the flower and fall, the sense of the profoundest secret depths of peace. Human life is so brief in its length, so calm in the valleys of the waves, so peaceful after its tears. For an instant that was longer than all his fifty years of life Hugh saw the one whole and inseparable peace in which sorrow is peace, and pain is peace, and the struggle of the oppressed against the oppressors is peace ; and every desperate throb of life is a ring of light, a ripple from the central heart of life, that is all life—the unending, indivisible, unchanging peace.

When Hugh left the church he walked quickly away. He felt no wish to talk to Allistair. He took the road that was leading down the hill towards Clere Crucis again. Time resumed its usual flow and the age-long moments passed now as moments. The morning was grey and the light clouded and uncertain.

But still each grass that rustled in the wind, each leaf, each thorn, seemed more clear than usual. The road dropped towards the valley. He knew now that his task was within his strength, that he could rebuild the church and reinspire the parish. Through Allistair he had drawn power from the very source of life.

He saw his own life in a new harmony : and the life of Underwood, and the dim unquenchable spark that had still burned in his failure and in the ruins of his church. He knew that he could never lose again that aspect of a more veritable world that he had for a moment seen. He knew that he had travelled himself, as in a tunnel, farther than he had ever thought.

Hugh paused and smiled, and found he had reached the ruined tangle of the Clere Crucis churchyard. Leaning over the wall, he read on a falling tombstone, half hidden by moss and drooping chains of ivy, the words :—

> 'All year long upon the stage,
> I dance and tumble and do rage
> So furiously I scarcely see
> The inner and eternal me.'

JOEY'S LAW CASE

With pegs in her mouth and her stout red arms stretched above her head, Mrs. Carter was busy hanging her washing on the line. It was a windy day and, as she struggled with the last billowing white sheet, she became aware that her next-door neighbour was watching her. Mrs. Carter pushed the last peg into position and turned round.

'Good morning, Mary,' said the other woman, coming to the fence.

'Good morning, Lou.' Mrs. Carter spoke a little shortly. She was not sure that she wanted a chat this morning. She couldn't abide other people shoving their oar in, and talking about her family. That was one reason, perhaps, why Mrs. Carter's line of washing, which ended in the garden, always began in the scullery, or even in the kitchen. There were some things you ought to be allowed to keep to yourself.

'I see your Joey's home again,' remarked Lou.

'That's right,' said Mrs. Carter. 'He's been at 'ome since last week.'

'Since last week,' said Lou reflectively. 'I only noticed yesterday as 'e was about.'

She waited hopefully and, finding Mrs. Carter did not offer further details, added, 'And left 'is wife behind too? Seems a pity he don't get on with her a bit better. I was saying to my 'usband only last night it seemed such a shame on you and Mr. Carter.

'Well, Lou,' said Mrs. Carter, 'there's two ways of looking at everything, ain't there? To tell you honest, I'm glad to have Joey away from her.'

'Reelly,' said Lou. 'You don't think she's ——' Her voice trailed off suggestively.

'I don't think anything beyond what my own eyes and sense can tell me; and that's something.' Mrs. Carter collected the unused clothes-pegs; then, hoisting the empty basket on her hip with one arm, she came slowly over to the fence. Perhaps it would be best after all to tell Lou her own mind about it, since people were bound to gas.

'Yes,' said Mrs. Carter, 'that girl Gracie ain't no good. She won't never make Joey a good wife, and often I've felt like praying as he could be rid of her, I have, really. The first time as I ever saw her I had my suspicions.'

'Your Joey was in the Guards Regiment then, wasn't he?'

'Yes, he was. And I wish he could 'ave stayed there. They won't 'ave them married below a certain age—and Joey was only twenty-one then. Well, he brings Gracie along home one day and when I sees the girl I ses to myself, "We'll be in for a peck 'o trouble with you my lady."'

'How was that, then?'

'Well,' said Mrs. Carter, warming to her subject, 'as soon as ever I clapped eyes on her, I ses to myself, "Ullo, my gal, you look a bit uncanny."

I haven't been a married woman these five-and-twenty years without knowing what *that* look means. "Well, come along in and take your coat off," I told her, and then as soon as she done that, I took a good look at her, and I thought to myself, "*Well*, Miss Gracie, if you ain't six months gone, *I* never 'ad one."'

'And you've 'ad ten.'

'Indeed, I 'ave,' replied Mrs. Carter with gusto. 'Well, that was a nice sort of start if you like. Not that I was judging her fer that, Lou; it ain't the first time that's 'appened and it won't be the last neither. But Mr. Carter was upset if ever a man was. "Don't you talk so, Dad," I told him, "it's as much your son's fault as it is hers anyhow, and the sooner Joey marries her and gets a room now the better, or we'll have 'er falling to bits in my front parlour one of these days." I wouldn't 'ave it put off, not another week.'

'Well, you surprise me, Mary,' said Lou. 'I'd no idea. Though I must say I thought the marriage was all rather quick and quiet. I did mention that to my 'usband.'

'I didn't mean you to have no idea either,' said Mrs. Carter, 'but since that's not the end of it by a long chalk, I'm telling you wot reelly 'appened.'

Lou nodded and made sympathetic noises with her tongue. 'That Gracie always seemed a nice enough girl to me,' she said. 'A nicely spoken girl I mean.'

'Too nicely spoken if you ask me. That soft

tongue of hers would talk anyone round. Oh, yes, I know what you mean well enough, Lou. Gracie talks like a lady. I'm quite aware of that. And she fancies 'erself a bit too; that's just half the trouble; she fancies she's too good for Joey. She's nothing but fag-smoking and drooping round. She was brought up to be a typist, and had a job in some office once, but what's the use of dwelling on that now? She wasn't too good for my Joey, when she felt like having a fling and wanted him for her fancy man. And she wasn't too good for him when she'd got herself into a mess and had a nice fright and wanted a husband, neither. What's the sense of playing the lady now? If only he'd never *started* with 'er!'

Mrs. Carter sighed heavily and looked round the yard. It seemed to her suddenly to be looking its worst; grey, damp, and ugly. She was always fighting for her family and they were always defeating her own efforts for their happiness in one way or another.

'And what's 'appened to Gracie now?' asked Lou.

'Just what I always 'oped would 'appen. She's left 'im and gone off to her people, and good riddance too. That's why I don't want people to go saying it's a pity they can't get on and why don't Joey take her back and all the rest of it. He's too weak; that's his trouble.'

Mrs. Carter returning to the kitchen, found Joey sitting by the fire. He was studying some piece of paper. He was doing piecework for a painter just now, and, this being the winter, things were slack. To look at him you would not have said Joey was weak. He was a hulking young fellow, well set up and schooled by drill. Like his mother's, his face was red and plump, but just now it looked lifeless and depressed.

'What 'ave you got there?' said Mrs. Carter, looking over his shoulder and seeing a bright pink form.

'It's a summons, Mum.'

'A summons! Good heavens, whatever for? Now, Joey, this is something as you haven't been straight with me about. What have you been doing?'

'It's not me,' said Joey.

Hastily taking the pink paper from him, she sat down and glanced through it. At the top she found the words, 'Petty Sessions.' The next thing that caught her eye was 'In the King's name.' In spite of the puzzle of legal phrasing, there was no mistaking what it meant. It was a summons to Joey to appear at the court at Aldershot for desertion of his wife.

'I don't see it. I don't see it,' she muttered again and again. 'It isn't right. It's been her doing all along. And then they summons you as if you'd been doing something wrong. What 'ave you done to be summonsed, I should like to know?'

Joey shook his head.

'She must 'ave been stuffing them up with some

lies or other. You can't tell what she might have said.'

'Well, Its downright wicked,' Mrs. Carter went on, 'after we've been so unscrupulous to do the right thing. Doesn't that go for nothing?'

Mrs. Carter had to hurry away. She had a busy day in front of her. She had a busy day every day. In addition to her own large household, she had a regular morning place, and gave help on two or three evenings a week at another.

Mrs. Carter was always ready to make any effort for the welfare of her family. And these efforts had meant hard work and more hard work. But here was a problem that hard work would not dispose of. A law case; Joey summoned before the magistrates because they'd said he had deserted his wife. And just when she thought that, by her forbearing and care to do the right thing, she'd saved him from all the unhappiness of his foolish wrong-doing with Gracie. How could work put it straight this time?

And when she got home that night, she found worse news still. Joey had had a letter from a lawyer, acting for Gracie; this letter told them it would be far better for them to settle the whole case out of court, and named a weekly sum, which Joey should pay to Gracie for her maintenance. The whole family, the girls, and all of them, thrashed it out time and again, till the alarum clock in the crowded little kitchen showed two in the morning.

'If you ask me,' Mr. Carter kept saying, 'the only thing is to pay and 'ave done with it all. No

Carter's never been in the courts yet. That's what we got to think of.'

'That's not sense, Dad,' said Mrs. Carter, 'we've just got to fight it. Why, it's as much as Joey makes in a week's work. Is the boy to have that hanging round his neck all his life?'

'It's no good,' said Joey, 'what can I do against a proper lawyer? I'm bound to lose.'

'Now that's silly talk,' said his mother, 'and quite enough of it. Come on, off to bed, you girls and all of you; its two o'clock.'

Mrs. Carter slept uneasily, and when she woke it was with a heavy reluctance. But she had a plan.

'Now, Joey,' she said, after the last breakfast had been hastily eaten and the last of the family bundled out of the house. 'You come and talk to me, while I wash up these things.'

While Mrs. Carter tied on her apron, Joey leaned against the draining-board and fetched a deep sigh.

'What you've got to find, Joey,' she said, 'is someone 'as knows about the law and that. What's the use of us conversing away, when we don't really know nothing about it? If that Gracie has got a lawyer putting her up to all the flim-flam, then you ought to have one too, didn't you.'

'How can I?'

'Well, you remember that young Mrs. Carvyll as I use to do for last year. Well, I was very good friends with her and young Mr. Carvyll was a lawyer and very clever at it too, I believe. I'm just goin' to ask her if Mr. Carvyll will 'elp you.'

'But how can I go dragging him all down to Aldershot? No, it ain't no good, Mum.'

'No, but you can have a talk with Mr. Carvyll one evening, can't you? And he could tell you what we're playing at, because I'm perplexed if I know.'

And Mrs. Carter was as good as her word. Snatching half an hour from her place, she panted round to Mrs. Carvyll. When she arrived home after her family had finished tea, she told Joey he was to go and see Mr. Carvyll at 8.30.

'I don't know what I can say to him,' said Joey, 'I shan't know 'ow to begin or nothing.'

'Oh, go and tell that to your grannie,' said his mother. So an hour later, with many fumblings and misgivings, Joey found himself in the Carvylls' sitting-room. His huge red hands fingered his hat. He shuffled before Mr. Carvyll, fourteen stone of melancholy awkwardness. Mr. Carvyll, assured and small, was not a whit older than Joey.

'Good evening, Carter,' he said, 'have a chair. Now, I'm sure we shall be able to straighten things out for you. First of all, let's see the summons they sent you.'

Joey groped in his pocket and, by the time he had found the summons, Mr. Carvyll had produced a quart bottle of beer and poured out two large glasses.

'Cheero!' said Mr. Carvyll.

'Good 'ealth, sir,' said Joey, and, after a draught, smacked his lips and began to feel more happy.

'This is simply a summons to appear at the court at Aldershot,' said Mr. Carvyll. 'Your wife apparently claims that you have deserted her—and you have to go and prove that that isn't true. What she wants to get out of it is a separation order from the magistrates, for you to pay her money to support her.'

Joey nodded his head.

'But the truth is that she left you after you had made her a perfectly good home. Now do you happen to have written her a letter since she went away, saying the home was still there if she chose to come back?'

'Yes, sir,' said Joey, 'my mother said I'd better do that.'

'Very wise,' said Mr. Carvyll. 'Now I wonder if you could remember the date on which you wrote and posted that.'

'Well, now. It must 'a been the Thursday after the Monday as she gone. That was the first evening I went round to our place.'

Mr. Carvyll began to make notes, and after he had put more questions of the kind to Joey, he read him out the points one by one; there were five or six of them.

'You're all right,' he said. 'There's your case, and, as far as I can see, it can't go wrong. Take this piece of paper and keep it.'

Joey took the sheet and studied it. Everything was labelled, headed, and numbered clearly and neatly. All the dates were written in. The whole thing was as plain as a pikestaff. Joey was amazed that Mr. Carvyll could have managed to make that neat little table in half an hour out of the tangle of happenings, which he had never seen plainly himself. He began to feel that with a man like this behind him he was safe.

'Now,' said Mr. Carvyll, 'I expect you feel all at sea about what will happen in court. So I'll tell you as much as I can about it, and exactly what you've got to do.

'When your case opens, your wife's lawyer will get up and make a speech. And when he's speaking, your job is to sit tight. He'll make you out to be the hell of a dirty dog; that's what he is there for.'

Joey grinned.

'But, whatever he says, say nothing; your turn comes later.'

'Oh, I 'as to make a speech after that?'

'You wait a bit, and I'll tell you. After your wife's lawyer has finished running you down, he'll put your wife in the box, and begin asking her questions. But of course he'll only ask her the questions she wants to be asked. But don't you worry about that. When that's over, you begin.'

'What do I 'ave to do?'

'You've got to say, "I want to examine the witness."'

'Well,' said Joey, 'I am glad I come to see you. I'm learning a thing or two.'

'Then your wife goes back into the box. Well,

don't get excited. Don't shout at her. Keep absolutely calm.'

'And I just asks 'er the questions as suits me?'

'That's the idea. Have the bit of paper I gave you ready, and just ask her the simplest questions you can to bring out those points.'

'And then do I go into the box myself?'

'Well, you can if you like; but you aren't much of a speechifier, are you?'

'I ain't too fluid.'

'Well, what I should like would be to have you call a witness to tell the story for you. How about your mother—she knows all about it, of course?'

'That's right, sir.'

'Well, make her go with you, and just let her go into the box and tell the story herself. She'd do that all right, wouldn't she?'

'I reckon she'd do it splendid.'

'Well, there you are. I know her, that's why I thought of it. And by the way, there's just one more question I meant to ask you. Since your wife left you, have you any idea that she's been with another man?'

'Well, since you ask it, Mr. Carvyll, yes. She'd left a letter from a man behind, and there's been another been returned to our address as she wrote him 'erself, which is both, well, *love* letters I should call 'em.'

Mr. Carvyll nodded.

'That just settles it,' he said. 'If you like to

bring that into your questions, the court may decide she's got no claim on you at all.'

After Joey had gone, Mrs. Carvyll said to her husband. 'I do hope it will be all right. It'll mean so much to Mrs. Carter.'

There followed for Mrs. Carter days of agonizing doubt. As she scrubbed, as she cooked, when she went to the pictures, even when she was bullyragging one of her girls for not wearing warm enough clothes, questions ground and ground their way through her mind. 'Will it be all right for Joey? Will he get rid of that good-for-nothing wife of his and be happy again?' How she hated all the talk and gossip that was going on: people judging Joey, and saying there were two sides to every tale. If only people hadn't got to keep shoving their oars in!

She could not gather much from Joey about his visit to Mr. Carvyll. She saw at least that it had given him some assurance. And she thanked heaven she was to go with him and speak for him. Oh, dear, if only it were over and Joey all right.

At last the day came, and Mrs. Carter and Joey were sitting together in an early morning train to Aldershot. Both were silent, Joey studying his paper of notes all the way. Mrs. Carter shivered from time to time and drew her old brown coat closer round her. At Aldershot they found their way through a grey drizzle to the court buildings.

'Where do we go now?' said Joey.

'I'll ask that bobby,' said Mrs. Carter, and showed the policeman the summons.

'Round the corner, ma,' he said, 'and through the yard.'

They crossed a rain-soaked gravel-yard and came to the court-room. Again they stood about, looking at the various doors marked, 'Witnesses,' 'Press,' 'Magistrates only.' A number of people were passing in and out, but no one took any notice of them.

'Well, what's the good of standing about getting wet?' said Mrs. Carter, 'I'm going in 'ere.'

She pushed through the witnesses' door, Joey following doubtfully.

At the entrance an official met them and led them into the court-room itself. Mrs. Carter had to sit in a different place from Joey, but she was sufficiently near to look at him and nod from time to time. Her eyes wandered round the discoloured walls and saw layers of grime. Those were the justices, she thought, sitting behind their raised bench at the end of the room ; and that one raised higher than the other in a sort of box must be the chief magistrate. Looking farther round the court-room, she saw Gracie sitting at a table with her solicitor. There was a thin, middle-aged lady in spectacles also at the table, talking earnestly to Gracie.

''Oo's that?' she whispered to a policeman standing near her. 'Is she a lady solicitor or something?'

'Bless you, no,' said the officer, 'that's Miss Sykes, the court missionary.'

Mrs. Carter now met Gracie's eyes. The girl, whose face was made up and who had a borrowed fur on, gave her a bold hard stare, without so much as nodding. The lady with the spectacles joined in the stare; no question that Gracie had got round her all right, artful little serpent. But even as Mrs. Carter was thinking what she'd like to say to her if she had the chance, she saw the case had opened. She leaned forward, straining to catch every word.

Now Gracie's solicitor was speaking. She could hardly believe her ears when Gracie went into the box to answer his questions. It was shameful the way he twisted everything round and made even the truth sound wrong. Even the visits that Gracie and Joey were always paying to her house and the help she'd given them were made to sound as if Joey had been unwilling to make a home of his own.

At last the lawyer finished, and after collecting his papers, he sat back with a satisfied air, as if the business were now entirely over. There was a slight hum of conversation; the magistrates were making one or two notes. Joey sat very still and, as Mrs. Carter watched him, her heart thumped in her throat. An usher motioned him forward.

As Joey stood up, you could feel a fresh stirring of interest in the court. How could this big, rough-looking young fellow manage his own case?

'I wish to examine the witness,' he said in a very low voice.

Gracie was recalled, and the court became silent and attentive. Joey stood with his sheet of notes in his hand, the notes Mr. Carvyll had written out for him. His first questions could hardly be heard, his voice was a bit shaky, but soon he took courage. At every question Mrs. Carter saw he was gaining ground ; the tissue of half-truth told by Gracie and her solicitor was crumbling away. Mrs. Carter was no longer anxious. She would never forget this scene. Her Joey so quiet and honest, speaking there before the whole room with everyone following. And this was her doing. It was his old mother at the back of him, who had found the plan and seen him through. He'd never have done it alone.

'There's just two more questions,' said Joey, 'Did you on the 10th April, before you left, have any letter from a man?'

'A letter from a man?' echoed Gracie. 'Well, yes, I may have had one that day.'

'Is this it?'

'Yes, I believe it is.'

'Will you read that out, please?'

Gracie took the letter, and looked imploringly round. At once the lawyer jumped up and made as if to take the letter from her.

'Really, sir,' he said, 'I protest against this. Quite beside the point surely——'

'Not at all,' said the magistrate sharply, 'we must hear it.'

But Gracie had had enough. She covered her face in her hands and burst into noisy sobbing.

'Kindly read the letter for her, Mr. Edwards,' the magistrate ordered, and the solicitor with a bad grace stood up. He glanced through the letter hastily, snorted, and read :—

'" My dearest little girl——" '

A hush fell on the court, and one after another sex-charged, blatant phrases were heard. After a few sentences the lawyer too had had his fill. He flung the letter down on the table, called out angrily, 'This is preposterous,' and sat down.

He then threw his papers into his bag, shut it with a loud snap, and turned his back on his client.

'Are there any more letters?' the chairman asked.

'Yes, one other, sir,' said Joey, 'but I'd as soon not 'ave it read out.'

'Quite right, Mr. Carter, kindly hand it up.'

The letter was passed along the Bench. Joey now asked if he might call another witness. Mrs. Carter found herself on her legs confronting the court.

She was not in the least nervous, as she saw the rows of faces turn towards her. She had not spoken at Dad's chapel meetings for nothing. Joey, she thought, had been almost too bashful and quiet, but she'd show the people she wasn't afraid to let her voice be heard on her son's behalf.

'Well, sir,' said Mrs. Carter, and at her first words people took a good look at her. 'I'm harsked to tell the court my story of my son's marriage. I suppose you'll be saying, as I'm Mr. Joseph

Carter's mother, I'll think 'e can't do nothing that's not perfect in my eyes. Well, I don't say 'e's perfect. No one's perfect as I ever met, but it's a funny thing as I come all the way from London to speak for him, and the railway fare means something to me, and neither of his wife's parents can't come in to court to say a good word for *her*, although they live in this very town. That strikes me as funny.'

'Mrs. Carter,' said the magistrate, 'you must stick to facts. Don't put in your opinions.'

'Well, that's the fact, sir, as I sees it,' said Mrs. Carter heartily. 'Now it's been said, I fancy, as when my son first got married he made no effort to provide a proper home, and they had to live in my house. But no one didn't mention *why* that happened. The truth was that the very first time as I saw Gracie, she ought to 'ave been married six months already. And it was my doing they fixed it up the very next week, all for her good, before the furniture was bought or we'd found a room. That's why there was those few months before the home was set up, but I got the bills in my bag now, and you can see we was buying pots and pans and furniture from that very week. And meanwhile the baby was born in my 'ouse and I had to turn out a good lodger.'

After Mrs. Carter had spoken for some minutes in this vein, and was getting into her stride, the justices thanked her and said they had heard enough evidence.

There was a buzz of conversation round the

court-room. The lay Bench conferred together, and presently the chairman rapped on his desk.

'There can be no doubt in the mind of anyone who has heard the evidence,' he said, 'that Mrs. Carter left her husband of her own free will, when he was supporting her properly. No fault lies with him and no separation order will therefore be granted. It is also my opinion from the evidence heard that no claim for maintenance could be granted by this court.'

Here was triumph! Mrs. Carter, laughing all over her face, jumped up and took Joey's arm and patted him on the back. She'd ridded him of that good-for-nothing drab for ever. Together they went out of the court-room and found sunshine sparkling on the wet ground outside.

'I say, Mum,' said Joey. 'I must speak a word or two to Gracie. I can't go without saying good-bye.'

'That's right,' said Mrs. Carter. 'Tell her we haven't got no ill will towards 'er. See that tea-shop across the road, I'm going in there and we'll have some dinner.'

She sat down at one of the glass-topped tables, and placed her bag in front of her. She had put aside two or three shillings for a good dinner. If things went wrong, they'd need it, she had thought and if things went right, they'd deserve it.

While she was deciding whether to have some nice fried fish or a good steak-and-kidney pudding, she could hardly help chuckling aloud. How splendid it was! She fell to thinking of Joey as a baby, as a little boy; the first day he went off to work at the factory; then as a fine young guardsman. And now he was hers again.

Joey came back and they ordered steak-and-kidney and cups of tea. After she'd finished, Mrs. Carter pushed her chair back and said, 'Well, Joey, what did you say to Gracie?'

'Well, I had a bit of a talk to her, Mum, and there was a lady with 'er, the court missionary.'

'Oh, yes, and what 'ad she got to say, I wonder?

'She said I ought to do a merciful act and take Gracie back. Gracie says her parents won't have her at home after all this, and she's got nowhere to go at all.'

'Well, that ain't our fault.'

'Well, this lady kept on saying 'ow can you leave a poor girl with nowhere to go, and it's your duty to take her back, she says; and if she done wrong once, the right thing was to give her another chance to do better; and she was sure she'd make me a good wife, and I ought not to be too judging and to show a Christian spirit and all to that.'

'Well, I like that. So you told her to mind her own business.'

Joey stared at the table as he answered slowly, 'No, I didn't. I told her I would.'

'What! You never mean to tell me as that court missionary persuaded you to take her back?'

'Well, what could I do, Mum? There was Gracie crying away and saying there was nothing for her but the streets, and this lady going on and on at me telling me it was my duty. I done it for the best. It's no good being angry with me.'

Mrs. Carter clenched her fists in her lap as her face went crimson.

'It's no good being nor doin' nothing,' she said. And after a pause she went on. 'I'd like to show that missionary some Christian spirit. What the 'ell does she know about our family affairs ? Can't I manage them myself?' Ain't I as good a Christian as she is?'

It was enough to break your heart, really it was. The whole box of bricks had been knocked down again. No sooner did her good sense and scheming get one of the family out of trouble than they went and put themselves right into it again.

And all the way back in the train Joey didn't dare say a word more. But Mrs. Carter talked a great deal. Again and again Joey heard her saying, 'Always shoving their oar in. Why will they shove their blasted oar in?'

Then, as the train drew in at Waterloo again, she calmed down and said, 'Well, Joey, I'll just have to have a set and think about it and find another way, that's all.'

THE YOUNG AGAINST THE OLD

It was certainly a marvellous beach that the boys had found for the picnic; a good half-mile of clear, firm sand, and not a soul about.

Two ancient cars drew upon the turf at the top of the beach, and nine or ten people and several children, with various picnic baskets, descended.

'This must be the place,' said James. 'There's old Dan sunning himself on the sand: what shall I carry, Mother?'

As they approached, Dan got up. He was an athletic-looking man in a black bathing dress, slightly built and brown all over from the sun: his hair was beginning to turn grey: so was the small moustache he had kept ever since the War. He looked like a captain or major living in retirement.

'Hullo, Dan,' said James, who was his brother. 'Where are those kids of mine?'

'Oh,' said Dan, 'still messing about in the surf: they tired me out an hour ago. What a thing it is to be young.'

'Ah, well,' said Mother. 'We can't be young all the time. Middle age has its compensations.'

The sea was right out, and a quarter of a mile or more away they could see the two boys wrestling with each other in the shallow water: their shouts and laughter came faintly across the blazing sunlit sands.

'It's astounding how they keep on the go,' said Dan. 'They've been in and out of the water half a dozen times: they've fought, and jumped, and wrestled, and they're still at it: I must say I admire it.'

James began bellowing for his sons to come and help find wood for a fire. By slow degrees, and with much horseplay, they approached. Both were brown from the sun—their fair hair showing bleached and almost colourless against their brown skin. Both were naked except for small red bathing shorts.

Rex was fifteen. Douglas twelve. Both were slim and speedy looking—like their Uncle Dan.

'Hullo, Dan, you old slacker,' said Rex. 'Pretty slack, aren't you: why didn't you stay down there with us?'

'Oh, I don't know,' said Dan. 'It was very nice up here.'

'You children can't keep Uncle Dan on the go all the time,' said their mother.

'Children!' said Rex. 'Call Douglas a child if you like, my good Mother. I shall be sixteen in September.'

'In sense and general behaviour I sometimes put you at about eight,' said his mother.

'In Latin, five would be nearer the mark,' said James. 'Rex, can you decline mensa yet?'

'I can decline to do anything,' said Rex. 'And anyhow I don't have any truck with the dead languages. Can I have a cigarette, Dad?'

'No.'

'Well, just one after lunch—you might as well let me, because I shall get it somewhere.'

'Don't show off, Rex.'

'All right, sorry—but we smoke at school, you know. Old Reggie caught me this last term.'

'Did he?' said Dan. 'What happened, Rex?'

'Oh, he just said I was a dam fool, and collared the packet, and smoked them himself: and he made me go for a training run to remove the ill-effects: not a bad scheme really.'

'Do you do anything else besides smoke at school nowadays?' said Dan.

'Oh, yes,—off and on.'

'Do you play any games?

'I'm rather good at marbles,' said Rex.

'Rex is turning into a runner,' his mother put in.

'Shut up,' said Rex. 'That's only silly.'

'What did he do?' said Dan.

'He won a race last term,' said Mother.

'Good man,' said Dan with interest. 'What was it?'

'Oh, nothing really,' said Rex. 'A thing they call the junior division mile.'

'Jolly good!' said Dan. 'That's the best news I've heard this week. Why didn't you tell me, Rex?'

'Oh, hell,' said Rex. 'You can hardly go and tell an ex-Olympic runner that you've just won a mile, under sixteen.'

'I'd no idea you knew *I* used to run,' said Dan.

'My dear old Dan,' said Rex. 'What do you take me for? If I've got it right, you were British mile champion for two years just before the War—and at the Olympic games a Finn beat you by a foot in the 1,500 metres.'

Dan nodded but he said nothing. He had been trying to make up that extra foot for twenty years.

'And everybody counted on you to win,' said Rex. 'What went wrong?'

'I could have won ——' said Dan, making patterns in the sand with one finger. 'I swear to this day I could have won. I made a b. f. of myself.

'What was it?' said Rex. 'Bad judgment?'

'I let him get away from me in the third quarter,' said Dan, 'by ten or fifteen yards. Then I failed to catch him, just by a foot.'

'It's that third quarter that counts,' said Rex. 'It's a question of even speed. That's how Jack Lovelock did his four seven.'

Dan nodded.

'That's the secret of the four minute mile, if you ask *me*,' said Rex. 'I bet somebody gets there soon.'

'What did you do for your junior mile?' said Dan.

'Oh, nothing—four fifty-nine—but it's only a grass track and I daresay it's been measured all wrong.'

'That's good,' said Dan. 'I never ran a mile as fast as that at your age.'

'Oh, well,' said Rex, 'since then.' He said *then*

as if he had been talking about the dark ages. 'All times have improved so much : people can run much faster nowadays.'

'I suppose they can,' said Dan.

'Rather,' said Rex. 'Think ; since your day the mile record has gone from four twelve down to four six. What was the best time you ever did for the mile actually, Dan?'

'Well, I think, it was four nineteen—the second year I won the championship.'

'There you are,' said Rex. 'You see they do four twelve two or three times every year now. My idea is this : I am going to get my mile down to four thirty during the next three years.'

'By the time you are nineteen,' said Dan.

'Yes,' said Rex. 'You see the great thing is not to overdo it when you are in your teens. I shan't aim for anything better, till I'm over twenty.'

'But, Rex—you won't be doing four thirty when you are only nineteen.'

'Why not,' said Rex. 'You didn't get a chance like we have nowadays. We get proper coaching right from the start. Barstow, who coaches at school, says he could train me down to four fifty or four forty-five now if he chose to, but it wouldn't be a good plan : there's nothing in it, really.'

'I doubt it,' said Dan. 'I don't believe you could run a mile in four fifty at your age. I should like to see you, anyhow. I wonder if *I* could run a mile in four fifty nowadays,' he added thoughtfully.

'Of course you couldn't,' said Rex. 'You must be over forty by now.'

'Damn you, Rex,' said Dan in anger. 'I bet I could still beat you at a mile anyhow. You seem to think it's all too easy. You talk of four thirty and four twenty as if you could do it without any trouble at all.' Dan felt annoyed. Rex was a fine boy and a handsome boy, but his assumption that he was in all respects an improvement on his father's and uncle's generation was not always agreeable.

'What's that?' said James, joining in. 'Are you offering to run young Rex off his legs? I wish you would, Dan. It might take him down a peg.'

'I've a good mind to try,' said Dan. He started trotting up and down on the firm sand, with a springy step, flexing his legs as he went. 'I don't feel too bad,' he said. 'I've a good mind to have a shot.'

'Go on, Rex,' said James. 'You race Dan over to the end of the beach and back, and see if he doesn't beat you easily.'

Rex looked self-conscious.

'No,' he said, 'what's the point? It sounds a bit silly.'

The other grown-ups joined in.

'Go on, Rex,' they all said. 'Show us how you can run.'

'Go on, Rex,' said Douglas. 'You're funking it.'

'It must be just about half a mile over to those rocks,' said James. 'It's a jolly good idea.'

'Wait a minute,' said Douglas. 'I've got my

bike here. I can measure out half a mile on my cyclometer and then put a mark, and they can run round it and back again.'

'Good idea,' said Dan. 'And you can take the times, James. Rex says he can run a mile in four fifty: I bet he can't.'

'Of course he can't,' said James. 'He thinks it's all too easy.'

'Dan, do take care,' said Mother. 'Remember you aren't used to this sort of thing.'

'I shan't hurt,' said Dan. 'I'll stop if I'm feeling the strain too much. I'll just go for a pipe opener.'

He set off at a brisk trot, and everyone watched him.

'He'll be all right,' said James. 'He's as hard as nails. He has been walking miles every day these holidays: and he plays squash and rackets regularly in London.'

After a few minutes Douglas rode back on his bicycle. He pointed to a boulder that he had dragged into position at the far end of the beach.

'It's exactly half a mile up to there,' he said, 'from this line. The sand's good and firm all the way.'

The party now gathered at the starting point—nine or ten grown ups and several young children. Douglas marked the starting line on the sand.

Dan walked slowly back breathing deeply as he came.

'All right,' he said. 'I'm ready.'

'I'm ready,' said Rex, 'if you really want to.'

They stood behind the starting line, both brown-skinned and almost bare : Dan in his black bathing dress and Rex in red shorts. Dan stood two or three inches taller than Rex, and he looked more solid all over.

Everybody watched in silence.

James pulled out his watch and waited for it to reach the exact beginning of a minute.

'Crikes,' said Douglas, 'this is quite exciting.'

A few seconds later they were off to a cheer. For the first hundred yards or so they kept even, then the lead went to Rex.

'Well run, Rex,' shouted Douglas.

The onlookers could now clearly see the difference in the runners. Dan's movements looked perfectly controlled and practised—his hips and shoulders travelled in a smooth straight line. There was a machine-like polish in his stride.

By comparison Rex was too loose and springy : his arms and elbows showed too much, but he ran so lightly and easily, that he almost seemed to blow along like thistledown in front of Dan.

Soon Rex began to draw away ; instead of being close on his heels, Dan was five yards behind—then ten.

'Well run, Rex. Well run, Rex,' cried the children shrilly, jumping about. The grown-ups looked on in silence.

By the time the turn came Dan was fifteen yards behind.

'Good for Rex,' shouted Douglas. 'He's winning easily.'

'Shut up, you little ass,' said James. 'The race hasn't begun yet: Dan knows how to judge speed.'

Half a mile away, now, they turned the boulder and began the homeward journey. The blue air was cloudless all round, the wide empty sands were dazzling to the eye. The runners looked small and doll-like in the distance.

'Rex started off much too fast,' said James. 'Dan'll come up on him now.'

In the meanwhile Dan had been having a very bad time. Directly he started he found the pace uncomfortable: his legs felt stiff and heavy, and he would dearly have liked to have set a slower speed. In a hundred yards he gave up trying to get the lead, and began to follow Rex.

He'll soon slack off, Dan thought; but to his dismay Rex seemed to keep up the speed without effort. After the first quarter, Dan, feeling puffed and tired already, had begun to let him go.

As they approached the half-mile mark, the beach sloped up slightly, and a fresh breeze, coming round the far point, met them head on. Dan found it harder and harder work and saw Rex leaving him at every stride. He cursed himself for having started.

As Rex turned the boulder Dan called out to him. 'All right, Rex. I'll have to stop,' but the wind carried his words back and away. At least

Rex never seemed to hear them. Dan laboured on after him.

Then as soon as he turned the mark, and had the wind behind him and felt the slight downhill slope, Dan began to feel much better. His muscles were warming up—quite suddenly he began to get back some of his old suppleness and joy of movement in running: his stride lengthened out powerfully and rhythmically. With each step, he felt coming back to him again the glorious timing and rhythm that it had taken him years of practice to perfect. Without noticing the violent pumping of his heart and lungs, he began to close up on the boy in front.

'This is great,' he said to himself. 'There's life in the old dog yet: I've still got something in me.'

Before they were half-way back to the finish Dan had caught Rex, and was running at his shoulder, stride for stride.

Now both grown-ups and children broke into loud excited cheering. James's eyes glistened with old memories as he saw his brother pulling a race out of the fire once again.

'Come on, Dan. Come on, Dan,' he bellowed.

'Rex—Rex—Rex—' yelled Douglas beside him.

To Dan's surprise Rex held off his challenge. He felt the boy was tiring and weakening: the beautiful lightness was leaving his action. He could tell from his breathing that he was having a bad time—yet Rex refused to let him pass. He found strength from somewhere to answer every increase in speed. Dan realized that he was up again a runner who'd fight him every inch of the way to the tape: his respect for Rex went up. He saw he was going to have the very devil of a race.

'I will beat him,' he said to himself. 'I'll show him.'

They were now about three hundred yards from the finish. They heard the little knot of people shouting at them. As the noise came to Dan's ears he forgot Rex and the bare empty stretch of sand. He saw himself coming round the last bend of a black ash track, with the green turf on his left: on his right an immense bank of yelling people: the roar of a huge excited crowd like thunder in his ears. He forgot the frenzied beating of his heart, the red-hot pain in his calves and thighs.

All he saw, a single stride in front of him, was the figure of the Finnish runner, whom he had dreamed of catching for twenty years. He felt his opponent stagger and weaken as he came up to his shoulder. He saw the tape stretched out only fifty yards in front.

With a wonderful sprint, still perfect in style, Dan came clean away from Rex, and crossed the line a good five yards in front.

James clapped him on the shoulder.

'Well run, Dan. Well run,' said James, grasping his hand. 'The time was just about four fifty.'

Suddenly Dan slipped down on to the sand and

lay motionless. As they looked at him, they saw his face and lips had turned a bluish colour.

Rex was the first to speak.

'Gosh,' said Rex. 'He's passed out.'

In the evening sunlight Dan lay without pillows flat on his back in bed. This was the only position in which he could breathe at all comfortably.

The local doctor turned from the bed and looked at James; then addressed them both.

He said: 'I suppose I had better be absolutely frank.'

'Carry on,' said James, with a grave face. 'Go straight ahead.'

'Well, it's your heart,' he said to Dan, 'you've damaged yourself pretty badly, but it doesn't mean you are knocked right out. You've strained it—just as you might strain a thigh or calf muscle. It's a thing which can get all right with great care and rest: you'll have to go very slow—very slow indeed for some years.'

The two brothers nodded.

'You must take care about violent exercise at forty and past,' said the doctor. 'It's worth it every time to watch your step. I didn't quite gather how this happened. You were running a race, weren't you?'

James explained.

'Why on earth didn't you let the boy win?'

'I don't know,' said Dan. 'It was silly of me: I got excited.'

'Oh, well,' said the doctor. 'I know it cheers us up to think we can beat the youngsters still; but it's not worth it. You'll have to take a week or so in bed, for a start. I'd better look in and see you to-morrow, and I think I'll drop a line to your own doctor in London.'

After he had gone Dan lay still: they had pushed his bed up to the window. He could hear the boys shouting and laughing in the garden directly underneath.

'Bad luck on old Dan,' he heard Douglas say. 'He's mucked up his heart or something.'

'Rotten,' said Rex. 'I feel it's all my fault too: I eased up so as to give him a race—If I'd left him standing he would probably have been all right. But I didn't like to.'

OLD HARD

About twenty miles from Bristol, where the last slopes of the Cotswolds look over the flats bordering the Severn estuary, there is a disused railway cutting. The lines and sleepers have been taken up for many years : grass and thorn bushes grow among the stones of the track.

On a summer evening a man dressed in blue trousers and a rough jersey with a roll collar was walking along this cutting. One side of the cutting lay in deep blue shadow, while the other was still alive with evening sunlight and gorse in bloom. The sailor looked carefully at each bank as he came along. Presently he saw in front of him a small black hut half-way up the side of the cutting, and he climbed up to it.

As he came round the hut to a small flat clearing, he found there was someone already there. The sailor drew back at once, not showing himself, but watching.

It was an old, frail man he saw, bearded, shaky in his movements as he laid out his things around him. He was settling down for the night. The sailor was close enough to see the pale smoke-blue yellow rimmed eyes of old age, and the ruined mouth working as he muttered to himself. The old man went on making his slow, hesitating arrangements, talking in an undertone all the time.

'O Lord,' the sailor heard him whisper, 'make me to know mine end and the number of my days. I have trodden the wine-press alone.' And after a pause he said out loud, 'Though man should live to fourscore years, then is his strength but labour and sorrow.'

'What's this?' thought the sailor. 'Some psalm-singing old cod? What's his lay?'

For some time he stood and watched. The muttering went on, and presently it seemed to change to cursing.

'Why can't you show me the way inside?' the old man said. 'Walking round all these bloody years—where's the way in—tell me that?' He was working himself up to a shout.

At that moment he looked up and saw the sailor looking at him round the corner of the hut. He stopped his cursing and jigging and sat down with a sigh. He stared down silently and fixedly.

The sailor came into the clearing, then sat down, loosened his boots, and began to take one or two packages from his pockets and lay them round him. As he did so they both watched each other under their eyebrows. It was the old man who broke the silence at length.

'Well,' he said, 'going to spend the night here?'

'Yes,' said the sailor. 'Any objections?'

The old man seemed to pull himself together and his voice grew firmer. 'No, I've got no objections.'

'Some years since I struck this spot,' said the

sailor. 'I wondered if I was going to find it. I've got a billy-can here to boil some water for a cup of tea; and I've got the tea; but what about the water?'

'Wait,' said the old man. 'What do you say to this?' He got up slowly and went to the hut. From inside he took an old overcoat and drew from the pocket a large bottle. He handed it over and the sailor read the label at arm's length. The cork had been pulled and replaced, and the bottle was about three-quarters full.

'Brandy?' said the sailor at length. 'Is this the real stuff? Liqueur? Cognac?'

'It's very fine,' said the old man. 'It cost me seventeen and a kick, and I found it in a village inn, where they had no right to have such stuff. It's a drink for lords.'

He sat on the ground again, slowly and stiffly.

'Look here,' said the sailor. 'Are you telling me you paid seven half-dollars for this, or do you mean that's what you *didn't* pay for it?'

'Go on,' said the old man in a listless voice. 'Drink up!'

The sailor pulled the cork and sniffed it suspiciously. 'Yes,' he said, 'that's the goods.'

Then he put the neck of the bottle to his mouth and took a deep gulp.

'Mary Ann!' he said, gasping. 'Mother's milk! Grand!' he jerked out between his gasps.

He took another drink and handed the bottle back.

'Put it on the ground between us,' said the old man.

'That's great,' said the sailor. 'My God, it is! Do you mean you really bought that!'

The old man motioned him to take some more. 'Take another one,' he said. 'You're a young chap, full of blood; you need it.'

'Not so much of the young chap,' said the sailor. 'I'm a damned sight nearer forty than thirty.'

'Just in the pride of life,' said the old man. 'Everything open to you. You've got your health and strength and the world with it; that's the point.'

'What do you mean?'

'You'll know what I mean one day; when you begin to lose it; when your friends begin to go, and things you've taken years to build up break down again.'

He took a pull at the bottle.

'Rollicking all done,' he said. 'Your joke's gone stale. Men talking a new language. I'm alone now, yet I don't die. What the hell's the use of that?' He took another pull at the bottle. 'Every time I lie down,' he said, 'I hope I shall never get up. Every time I wake up and find I'm still alive, I curse because I'm not dead.'

He passed the bottle over to the sailor, who took a long pull.

'By gosh, it's good!' he said, and gave a long, contented sigh.

The old man took the bottle back and drank

again. He went on talking, holding the bottle up in the air.

'Sometimes I kick the ground,' he said, 'and knock it with my head.'

The sailor stared at him, then took the bottle from him and drank deeply again. He put the bottle down and they fell to eyeing each other in silence.

It was now about seven o'clock. Not a cloud had been seen all day, and to the west the shining waters of the Severn estuary merged with the liquid golden light of the sun, as it sank. The faintest touch of chill was creeping into the air. It came up from the glinting waters of the estuary, touching their cheeks with freshness, and bringing a hint of salt and damp to their nostrils.

'So you're making for Bristol?' said the old man.

The sailor began to speak but stopped. 'What the hell are you talking about now?' he said. 'Who said anything about Bristol?'

'Well, I was only working things out a bit. You're not long off a boat, are you?'

'No.'

'And if you're walking anywhere from London or Southampton, you wouldn't have got here.'

The sailor said nothing.

'Well, I suppose you've been walking down from Liverpool; and you're making for Bristol.'

'Yes.'

'And at Bristol I expect you're going to look round for someone for a while?'

The sailor glared at him. 'Don't ask questions, he said, 'or you might get a knock on the nut.'

'Don't take offence,' said the old man. 'Nothing to be offended at. I go alone so much, I get talking; that's all. It's plain to me you know the way round here, or you wouldn't have come slap to this hut and, if you know the West as well as that, I only thought you would be visiting someone along in Bristol. Now aren't I right?'

'Well, since you ask,' said the sailor, 'and to give you a polite answer, mind your own bloody business. I should.' Wish I'd never mucked in with the old doodle, he thought. Why can't he shut up?

'A man like you doesn't run round the country looking for the end of a rainbow,' the old man went on, making him writhe with impatience. 'Think I'm an old fool, don't you? Now listen to me for a moment. When I see you three weeks off a boat, making straight for Bristol, *Trimmer Wylie*, I ask myself what it's all about.'

In an instant Wylie was at his throat, throttling him and shaking his head backwards and forwards. 'You say that,' he said, 'and I'll wring your bloody neck a yard long.'

He loosened his grip and gave the old man room to breathe, but still held him.

'You go on if you like,' the old man said in a shaking voice. 'I shan't mind if you do me in. But I advise you not to; because you'll never know, then, what I've got to tell you.'

Wylie let him go. 'Who the hell are you?' he said. 'I don't know you.'

'Don't you get worried,' said the old man. 'I'm a friend of yours.'

Wylie stared at him. Then in a second he was wringing his hand and putting an arm round his shoulders.

'By Jeeze!' he said. 'Old Hard! What a fool I am. Put it there!'

'That's right, Wylie,' said the old man, smiling. 'Alexander Hard himself. It does me good to see you. It makes me feel younger already.'

They went on pumping each other's hands, both feeling a bit on with the brandy by now.

'Forgive my being rough with you,' said Wylie. 'But who could have known you this way, beard and all. And you were so clever, too. You gave me a scare. Three weeks off a boat and making for Bristol! You're right; but as far as anyone else is concerned, I'm gone for ever. All that's known about Trimmer Wylie is that he got a boat to South America; and he got mixed up in a row there and very likely got knifed. Anyway, he's never been seen again.'

'But why?' cried Hard, 'what's the advantage? Trimmer Wylie was a name that carried some weight, and there was more use in it than danger.'

They looked at each other and felt the drink warming their hearts. The sun was setting lower and filled the whole air with a soft, brandy-coloured glow. They made themselves comfortable against the sheltered side of the black tarred hut and began to drink again. Wylie took out a packet of cold meat and bread, and made a meal. The old man refused food altogether.

'It must be ten years since I saw you,' he said. 'I heard about you for a few years from that London lot, then you just disappeared. It does me good to see you again, Wylie. It brings things back again. What are you thinking of doing now?'

'I'm going to marry and settle down.'

'Have you made your fortune?'

'No, but I'm just going to.'

The old man paused, waiting for him to speak. Wylie took a pull at the bottle.

'Look here, Hard,' he said, 'you're just the chap I want. You can still do a bit, I suppose?'

'I might.'

'You might find a place for some jewellery, precious stones; things like that?'

The old man nodded. 'I'm not quite dead yet,' he said. 'Where are they?'

'Well,' said Wylie. 'Listen, and I'll tell you.'

'When I was in London, I got in with a queer crowd round Tottenham Court Road; that part of the world; and in the house I lived in there was all kinds of trade thriving. Dope was one of the best lines they had. There were two or three girls living up on the top floor. There were a few young lads who made a special job of knocking suitcases off cars, and there was a chap called Bernstingl who's a first-class man on anything to do with jewels. He knew where everything was that was worth anything in London.'

'I knew him at one time,' said Hard. 'We've done a bit of trade together.'

'Well, I hope you kept your end up,' said Wylie. 'He was a proper Yid, and a swine.'

'I managed,' said old Hard. 'I heard about you from him too sometimes.'

Wylie nodded. 'It's good to see you like this,' he said. 'Give me that bottle. Well, I used to take a boat from time to time, and I used to go back and work in with these chaps again and, being anxious to improve myself, I learned a lot.'

He chuckled.

'There was only one thing against it; that chap Bernstingl liked to regard himself as a kind of boss, and if it comes to working for a boss, there are plenty of safe jobs. I meant to stay a year or two to learn what I could; then come back down this way and pick up with you again. I always liked you. I thought one day I might fit in pretty well with you, and you might give me a leg up on your side.' He looked at Hard, and Hard gripped his hands; they shook hands for some moments in silence.

'Did you?' said Hard, with a new eagerness in his voice. 'Say that and you make me feel I have a life to live yet. I always looked on you as a sort of son. I've always been watching for you to turn up again some day.'

The bottle passed.

'I had some guts in me too when I was young,'

said Hard, 'and I looked to see you again. And now I see you, I'll tell you what I feel.'

'That's all right,' said Wylie, and he nodded.

'Well, one day this chap Bernstingl wanted me to go on some special job ; some well-known actress who'd got a necklace in a friend's house. Bernstingl had planted a girl in the house, as a maid. All I had to do was to slip in one night, take the jewel box from the arranged place and pick out the necklace. That was all right. Only things began to take a funny turn. I had a curious feeling, so I beat it. I did the famous vanishing act.'

Hard nodded.

'I had a feeling,' said Wylie. 'I get them. If I didn't trust my own feelings, I shouldn't come through as well as I do. About two days after that, Bernstingl got himself into a mess. They knew all about our little lot. But I had already hopped it. And I had the prize picking. It was worth thousands.'

'What did you do?'

'What did I do? I kept my head, of course. I was on a boat for South America two days later. My seaman's papers were all in order—they always are—Trimmer Wylie, that's all I've been for the last four years. But now I thought was the time to come home and live on my earnings. Now things will have died down.'

It was now dark, and Wylie turned and looked seriously into the old man's face. 'Look here,' he said. 'What I'm after is this. If you had a necklace like that now, would you still be able to do anything with it?'

Hard had a good gulp of brandy and laughed aloud.

'Wylie,' he said, and he laughed and cried at the same time. 'I praise God for this night. I've got a life to live yet, I see. I thought I was broken down and alone. Let me have those diamonds, and we'll work together on the old scale. I'll place a stone here and a stone there slowly. I said you'd come to Bristol to look for someone, and you've met the one man in the world you were looking for; that's me.'

Wylie nodded. 'That's true,' he said. 'You take some beating at your end of the game; I can trust you.'

'Where is the necklace?' said Hard.

'We're damned near it now,' said Wylie, 'and we're going to get it to-night. Give it an hour or two till the moon's up. But what the hell's been happening to you? Why the tramp rig-out? What's gone wrong? What's happened to the pawn-shop and your family?'

'My wife's dead,' said Hard.

'And what about the shop?'

'Well, things went wrong, and I had to leave that place quick and get away. Then, every time I had an address and started up, they were after me. So what could I do? I had to keep on the move if I wanted to do any trade, and I've been keeping on the move ever since. That's how I work it. I meet people all over the place, you see. When they want the red stuff, quick and ready, I give it them, and I take what they've got. But it's not much good. Just a pound here and a pound there. What's that to me? And I've been lonely. I'm too old for this sort of thing.'

He shook his head and sighed deeply.

'I don't fear death, Wylie,' he said. He smote on the ground with his stick. 'I knock on death's door and it never opens to me. In my old age I've become a byword and a thing of shame. You get these thoughts when you're old and deserted.'

Wylie nodded his head slowly as old Hard rambled on.

'Well,' he said, 'the brandy's nearly gone. Let's finish it up. There's a lot in what you say. These last few years I've been feeling that way myself. I'm going to marry and settle down if you can fix things up. It's all up to you. I might get a village pub somewhere, and you could live nearby—I'd take care of you and look after you.'

Then the old man rose up in the darkness and, drunk as he was, fell on his knees and kept thanking God for giving him such joy and calling him back from a living grave of sorrow and bringing Wylie to comfort him.

Wylie laughed contentedly as he lay on his back on the grass.

'Go it!' he said, as the old man went on. 'I bet God arranged it all for you,' and he laughed again.

Presently they both fell asleep.

An hour or two later the pebbled margin of the Severn estuary crunched beneath their feet. A brilliant moon was now high in the sky and the water stretched silver and black before them.

'This is the place,' said Wylie. 'Walk carefully, it's rotten everywhere.'

They set foot cautiously on an old disused wooden pier that ran out into the water. At its far end, and lying some hundred yards or so out, was a battered hulk of a boat, lying careened on a sandbank. The moon shone over the tangled rigging and splintered gunwale and the water glittered as the current rippled round the hulk.

They picked their way cautiously along the wooden jetty, trying the wooden planks with their feet.

'That's it,' said Wylie. 'If we came here in daylight, there's no knowing who might not see us. That old boat's lying on a sandbank. Just behind it there's dry sand at low tide. I've only got to go out there and get the tin case out of the boat. It's as safe there as your own private bank deposit. I know the chap who owns her.'

The black silent current slipped by their feet. It ran swiftly beneath them through the wooden piers, curling and bubbling straight out into the channel beyond.

'It's a hellish tide,' said Wylie. 'I never knew it run so fast.'

They stared at the water.

'I'll tell you what it is,' he said. 'This sand's

shifted or something. I waded out before. That's deep water now ; and it's running like hell.'

'Doesn't look too safe to me,' said Hard.

'I shall have to swim for it,' said Wylie.

For a little while they argued. Both agreed it was going to be a dangerous job with the strong current. But Wylie, still inflamed by the brandy, insisted on going. He took off his clothes and lowered himself into the water.

'It's hellish strong,' he called out. A moment later he had disappeared into the darkness.

The tide was running along shore, moving from the wreck towards the jetty, so that Wylie was swimming almost dead against it. But the current also bore strongly outwards, off the shore. It coiled and sucked round the piers of the jetty and at its far end a silent swirl of black water raced like a smooth stream out and out into the darkness.

Hard saw that Wylie ought to swim straight from the wreck back towards the shore, otherwise the outwards current would catch him when he was tired and sweep him past the end of the jetty away into the darkness. He waited, pacing backwards and forwards many times, and staring at the water. At last he heard a faint call from the darkness. Wylie was coming back.

'Make for the shore,' shouted Hard in desperation. 'Don't make for this end of the jetty.'

He waited and waited. No answering call came. He went to the end of the jetty, straining to see into the darkness.

At last he saw the white gleam of Wylie's face and shoulders in the path of moonlit water about twenty or thirty yards off. He knew at once the exhausted efforts of a weak swimmer. Inch by inch Wylie came nearer. Then the current held him; held him as firmly as if he had been tied with ropes. He was so near the jetty now that Hard could see his face in the darkness.

'Can you do it?' he shouted.

Wylie made no answer. His face was set and desperate. He had no strength to speak to Hard but only to fight the current. He came within twenty yards of the jetty, then he seemed to stay fixed, struggling there in silence, unable to gain another hand's breadth.

'Let yourself go,' shouted Hard. 'Get back to the boat.' But at that moment the off-shore current took him. Suddenly Wylie began to move outwards past the end of the jetty. He tried to shout now. But only a gurgling, stifled cry came to Hard. Instantly Hard plunged into the black waters himself. He swam frantically this way and that, calling. But only the current raced by him silent and eddying, carrying him far out into mid-stream. Very soon he was exhausted. He swam out into the darkness with dull despair; then, as if he were falling asleep, long waves of drowsiness overcame him and carried him away.

Later Hard awoke to find his face pressed against stones and wet sand. He walked, staggering. Rosy light filled the air and a dawn wind began running along the grasses. Presently he saw Wylie lying on the beach just clear of the water. His face was grey-blue. Hard saw that he had been drowned some hours ago. His hand still gripped the chain of diamonds.

Hard picked them up, looked at them without interest, and flung them aside. Then he stared at the sodden, dishonoured body of his friend lying at his feet.

'Wylie,' he said, 'Wylie.'

Then he began to run across the beach, stumbling as he went. He ran a few yards, then cast himself down on the grass that came almost to the water's edge. He pressed his lips and mouth into the broken sandy earth and the yellow shoots and knots of grass.

'Let me in,' he moaned to the earth. And then in a voice that rose to a wail, 'Let me in. Let me in. Let me in.'

MAY-DAY CELEBRATIONS

It would be about now they would be coming, Mabel thought, and her heart beat somewhat faster. Thomas's face was all about her, wherever she turned; changing, changing from the boy with black hair and violent ways to the elderly man with the patient look; the waiting look; and the eyes deeper and deeper set with something in them of failure, and something in them of sticking to it.

Now she saw the red and white cheeks he used to have in his 'teens; now the grey face with heavy lines, and the stubble turning grey, and the shaggy eyebrows—and his eyes, which looked tired.

She heard the band now in the distance—the marchers were coming into the gardens. The crowd grew more dense every moment, and tremors of excitement shuddered through it, like gusts of wind in high corn. Mabel was carried sideways against her will over towards the platforms and the banners. A dense crowd was waiting there for the marchers and the speakers.

There were two platforms under the trees at the corner of the gardens. Round them the red banners were stretched. Overhead clouds were racing in a stormy sky, and the branches threshing and weaving in the wind.

Mabel found herself carried in the crowd into

the arms of an old friend. The two women greeted each other.

'It's a good muster,' said Mabel. 'The numbers are very good.'

'Who's going to speak? Is your husband speaking?'

Mabel shook her head.

'He's going to start it off,' she said. 'He's taking things a bit easy. This fellow Hardy's going to speak.'

The crowd was massed solid round the platforms now, and policemen's helmets seemed to float everywhere among the heads. And beyond the crowd she could see the heads and shoulders of mounted policemen gliding about. Mabel knew there were almost as many policemen as there were demonstrators and marchers. There always were at a big meeting.

There came a wavering cheer, taken up uncertainly here and there: and the marchers began to file past the platforms. On each side of them marched a rank of policemen. Mabel saw first the bobbies' red faces, purple and red with the full blood of health—and their red, fleshy necks and their upright carriage; each man of them carrying his twelve and fourteen stone like a boy athlete. She saw beef as they went by: and roasting fires. She saw steaks sizzling in grills and frying-pans. She saw gravy, and crusty chunks of bread and butter and foaming pints of beer and stout.

Then she saw the marchers; and she was watching pale, ill faces, grey and yellowish : she saw the dragging feet and ragged clothes. Here and there a man squared his shoulders and stuck his jaw out. In every face she saw sadness and old despair : she saw the drawn lines that she had seen so often, and the patient, stern look of the men who were brave. She saw rain-soaked street corners, and men leaning motionless against street posts with the rain drifting over the cobble-stones. The word *hunger* transfixed her like a spear, a pain that ached in her own body. Hunger marchers, she thought—men who marched under the banner of Hunger. They were hungry: and they marched because there was nothing else for them to do.

Leading a section, her Thomas passed, looking steadfastly ahead. She pushed her way with purpose now towards the platforms. Thomas mounted the platform and held up his hand for silence. A hush fell.

For a moment or two he looked about him at the marchers. What were his feelings? Mabel knew he was not thinking of himself, nor of her, nor of anything but of them. As he waited and looked from one side to the other a low mutter of recognition began to arise ; it was a rough growl of friendship that never rose to a cheer : something more friendly than a cheer. Thomas's grave deeply lined face looked round on the crowd, and he held up a strong, square hand.

'Comrades,' said Thomas, with slow Lancashire emphasis, 'you know me well. You know something of what I have done for you in these thirty years. I wish it were more,' he suddenly cried, 'by God I wish it were more.'

A sudden silence spread now.

'I'm not come here to speak for myself,' Thomas went on more calmly. 'I want to present to you Mark Hardy. He has been to Russia. Once he talked with Lenin himself. He is going to speak of our plans for the coming year.'

Hardy stood up. He was a man of about thirty-five—over six feet. His face was thin and handsome, with deep-set eyes. His hair was black and untidy. He wore a black coat and trousers and a red shirt open at the throat.

Before speaking he suddenly flung off his coat—and held his two arms towards the crowd. The murmur of talk round the platform died away. He began to speak at once swiftly and in loud, clear tones that carried far and compelled the attention.

'Friends,' he said, 'comrades—fellow workers. During the last five years we have passed through a century of experience in our long struggle : events have moved : and we have made a tremendous advance towards the inevitable downfall of capitalist misrule, and the building up of the workers' united and world-wide front.

'In this five years we have seen every capitalist country sucked far down in the economic maelstrom. We have seen their foundations splitting and cracking. We have seen the feverish and insane efforts of Nazi and Fascist reactionaries in their despairing effort to shore them up.'

Mabel's mind began to wander: now she had seen the marchers and heard Thomas speak, she began to edge away towards the back of the crowd.

Presently a burst of applause called her mind back to the speaker. Hardy was saying:

'We are asked this year to celebrate King George's Jubilee. You know as well as I do that all this Empire hullabaloo in the lickspittle press is propaganda: cold-blooded propaganda, aimed to divert peoples' eyes from the sickening state of present affairs.

'What have we in truth to celebrate? First that after twenty-five years of the present reign we accept that millions of men in every capitalist country continue in permanent unemployment. A glorious achievement indeed! Millions of workers condemned to a standard of life that would be despised by primitive savages. Secondly, we celebrate that since 1926 Trade Unions have been placed in a weaker position than they have occupied since the days of Castlereagh, and the Six Acts. Another great capitalist victory! Thirdly, that England continues to exploit by bloodshed, force, and cruelty the Asiatic nations. Fourthly, that insane quarrels over the ill-gotten Imperialist gains among the nations lead us to the very brink of another horrible war, to which the workers will once again be driven: a war which brings to the workers nothing but torture, degradation, horror. And the next war will carry every fiendish device of slaying and torture into the workers' own homes among their women and children.'

Hardy poured all this out in a torrent of clear and unhesitating speech. Suddenly he paused and looked round. Then he went on with slow measured emphasis :

'Stop it : stop it before it is too late. Remember Invergordon. Think of the power of the massed will of the people, the same needs, the same enemies in every country. There is no hope for you in nationalism. . . .'

While he was speaking the sky darkened : clouds and gusty rain came spinning through the air. The trees swayed, and men tightened their collars round their throats.

'Let's go,' said Mabel to Beth. 'Let's get back. I'd like to have some tea ready when Thomas comes in. He'll need some warming up.'

They slowly edged their way out of the crowd. When they reached its distant scattered fringe, they turned round and looked back. The outer groups of people were talking together : many were breaking off and going away as the rain came on. From here the voice of Hardy could still be faintly heard.

'This form of state will go : be assured of it : *war* will go . . .'

Nearer in round the platform the crowd pressed silent, unmoving. Mabel looked back at the platform, and saw Hardy using his arms as he spoke, though his voice no longer reached her : and she saw Thomas sitting beside him : and the crowd packed round them.

The platform seemed like a heart or core of life, sending its own pulse through the silent, waiting crowd that pressed round to drain life from it. Her mind became filled with the image : she saw it as a brazier of coals in the dark, and men pressing round it, with the light gleaming on their hands and faces and clothes : she saw it as the pay office at the mills when she was a girl, with scores of men struggling round to draw their money. She saw it as a multitude of flowing, changing pictures, with light breaking through the clouds. She saw it as a stone sending silent ripples across the surface of a pond.

Both women were silent as the 'bus took them away from the parks and shopping streets to the grime-covered parts of the town beyond the two railway stations, where there were factories and warehouses and poor men's homes.

Mabel led the way through the dark arches which carried one of the stations above the streets and houses. They came out into a street of small houses, which lay for ever under the shadow of the enormous viaduct. Their walls were crusted with sooty deposit, so thick that it fell away at the touch of a hand. The air was filled with smoke, white, grey, and brown. And the little houses shook to the unending clamour of the trains overhead.

Mabel led the way up a bare boarded passage

and uncarpeted stairs: the walls of the passage were thick with railway grime. She had two rooms. When they got inside, Beth looked round at the linoleum, worn and polished, and at the bareness of everything. She was used to rooms in which beds and tables and upholstered chairs jostled against each other.

'We've got another room here,' said Mabel. 'This is only the sitting-room.'

She hung her mackintosh and hat on the door: she stooped down and put a penny in the gas meter and lit a small gas-ring for the kettle. They settled themselves to talk. They sat with their knees apart and their hands resting in the outspread laps. Mabel and Beth had led hard lives; but time had brought their bodies a roundness which gave a placid dignity to all they said and did.

'It's a grubby place, this,' Mabel said. She began to put out cups and plates. 'I hope you'll overlook my not spreading a cloth: it'd only be black by the end of tea. The blacks get in even with the windows shut.'

As she spoke a long goods train rumbled past, filling the room with clanking.

'I don't like living in Railway Street,' she went on. 'It ain't exactly my idea of a country cottage with nice roses to smell. But Thomas has got to find a place for his little printing press. It's what they call a platen. We can put it down in the basement on a stone floor here. It's not every street they'd let you have a printing press.'

'Does he print the *Worker's Clarion* on it?' said Beth.

'No; it wouldn't take that,' said Mabel. 'That's got much too big an affair—which is all to the good. But they want him to issue a lot of small pamphlets all the time.'

She opened a cupboard door and showed, instead of cups and saucers, piles of papers and pamphlets. A cascade of papers came sliding out on the floor: they began to fall from the shelves, manuscripts, printed sheets, blank paper, all confused together.

'What do you think of that for a larder?' said Mabel.

Beth shook her head.

'Well,' she said, after a long silence, 'you would have him.'

Mabel pushed the papers back into the cupboard, moved another pile from a wooden chair, and sat down.

'Don't think I meant that for a complaint against Thomas, or the way we live,' she said. 'You're right. I would have him—and perhaps my people were doing right in trying to stop me. I was only nineteen. But I've never lived to regret it. I was quite right, Beth, young as I was. There are some things the young ones know. He's a good husband and a good man: and I say that after forty years of married life. What more can a woman say than that? How many can say that much?'

Beth nodded.

'Forty years, is it? We're getting old. I can remember it all so clear, too: as if it was only last year. It seems funny.'

They both fell to thinking of other days and times, far-off scenes, when they were young slim girls in white muslin who ran with flying feet; who were caught by the waist on summer nights.

Mabel began to put out a loaf and butter on the bare table top.

'You'll stay and have a bite, won't you?' she said. 'We don't live very high: but there's some bread and butter and jam: the butter's as cheap nowadays as the marge.'

'Unless you have the fivepenny marge,' said Beth.

Mabel went on talking as she set out the tea with slow, quiet movements.

'Mind you,' she said, 'my married life hasn't been all honey and jujubes. I'm not complaining. Why should I? But when a man lives for something beyond the ordinary things of life, home can't be his be-all and end-all.'

Beth nodded.

'That's it,' she said.

Mabel paused with a plate in her hand. 'But take yourself, too,' she said. 'It cuts all ways. Your Arthur's been a good steady worker always. But you haven't been too happy with him.'

Beth nodded again.

'To all outward appearance,' Beth said, slowly and decidedly, 'Arthur looks like a 'usband to be proud of. But there it is. I got my crying over early in my married life. I did plenty of it then. He's a bully, that's the trouble: and he's never thought for anyone but himself. He's selfish to the bone. The first ten years of my marriage were all babies and black eyes.'

'There have been times when I've felt it hard, too,' said Mabel. 'I've never had what I should call a home. Never in all these forty years. I've had to see my young ones go hungry and cold, when they were little. And I've never been able to give them a farthing to help them now they're older. We never know where we may be from one week to the next. Years ago I used to cry, too, when Thomas's views and meetings kept getting him the sack from good jobs. Many's the time I've said to him, "What's the use of going on?" Then every time he got a new job I used to think to myself, "Now I'll have a proper home." But just as we was getting things together something always went bust. We've lived in fourteen different towns, let alone all the rooms: they're more than I can remember.'

'But he's settled in a good job now, isn't he?' said Beth. 'He's been there for a year or two.'

'Yes, we're really better off now than we've ever been yet. I'm really beginning to hope now that I'm going to get a home together. We'll be out of this pig-sty in a year. Thomas is beginning to take it easier now. He doesn't do so much—not all day and every day, like he used to.'

'Well, he's getting on in years,' said Beth.

'Yes, he says he feels he isn't in the forefront any more: he looks to leave things to the younger men. But he can still earn good money. He always could. He's a foreman compositor now on the *Morning News*—working on the advertisements. It's a good job. I'm beginning to think we'll settle down yet, Beth: I'll be asking you to see me in a nice little place one of these days, in a little peace and comfort.'

Beth nodded.

'I'm sure I need it,' said Mabel. 'The kettle's on the boil now. I'll make tea. If he's late, I can make some fresh.'

'Is that the fourpenny,' said Beth, 'from the Stores round the corner?'

'It's the threepence-halfpenny. Tell me what you think of it. The only thing I wonder is whether he'll ever be happy if he gives it up. His one grumble has always been 'e's never been able to do enough for the *cause*. He's said that every day for the last twenty years, I should think.'

'What did you think of that fellow's speech this afternoon?' asked Beth.

Mabel sat silent for a little while.

'He seems a nice enough man,' she said at length.

'Yes, but what about all that he was talking about?'

'I don't know quite what to make of it,' said Mabel. 'And I've heard enough speeches in my time. He always talks that sort of thing. He means it when he says it. But I don't quite trust it somehow. What's he got to do with it all? He's a chap with a lot of money behind him. In Thomas's young days it was a fight against the *owners*: men understood what they were making for—and knew who was against them. Thomas spoke to the men about their own towns and factories and homes, and what they'd better do next week: not about the whole of this world and kingdom come. I sometimes think speech-makers like him get so full of the new plans in front of them and all to that, they forget what these poor fellows want is just food and dry clothes.'

'But he's an important man, isn't he?' said Beth. 'He's been an M.P. hasn't he? He'll be somebody one of these days.'

'Yes, I daresay he'll be someone,' said Mabel, 'on one side or the other. But it can't mean the same to him as it did to my Thomas when he was a young man. Yet he pushes forward and takes the limelight—and Thomas takes a back seat.'

'Well,' said Beth, 'you oughtn't to mind that: only a moment ago you were saying you'd be thankful if only he would drop out of things a bit and keep a steady job for once.'

'Yes,' said Mabel, 'but sometimes I feel—seeing all the work he's done—giving his whole life to it—he deserves something a bit more out of it.'

'You persuade him to give it up,' said Beth, 'and have a little peace and quiet for once in your life. I saw a little house out our way in Welcome's Fields a week back. You could have got it on the money he's making now. Let him spend it on you and his home for once.'

Mabel drew breath and compressed her lips: then she let it out as a slow, thoughtful sigh.

'We'll see,' she said. 'We'll see what happens.'

'It's time you had your way for once,' said Beth. 'You take my advice.'

'Here he is,' Mabel said.

They heard his footsteps in the passage, then on the bare boards of the stairs.

Thomas came in and greeted his wife and Beth a little absently. He sat down on a chair with a grunt. He was dressed in a dark serge suit with a muffler at his neck. His grey hair was closely cut and his face, once full of fire and expression, had grown dour and set and stubborn.

'I'm getting old,' he said.

'That's just what we've been saying,' said Beth. 'We're all getting old.'

'I'll just have time for some tea,' said Thomas, 'then I want to get down to the paper. I shan't be back till we've put her to bed. I'll be back about one. Then I shall have a full day on to-morrow, till late again. I had to work it that way so as to get off this afternoon.'

'You'll be worn-out,' said Mabel.

'It won't be the first time,' said Thomas.

Beth said: 'You ought to think of your health a bit more at your age.'

'I've got better things to think of,' he said.

'Not for Mabel.'

Thomas ignored her answer. Presently she said good-bye and went.

'I wanted to get downstairs to-night,' Thomas said, 'We want another thousand of those Invergordon pamphlets. That's been doing good work. But I can't manage it now—it's too late. Then they're asking me to do Hardy's speech later on. My Vanguard Press is getting well known.'

'What did you think of that speech of Hardy's?' said Mabel. 'I only heard the first part.'

'It was good,' said Thomas. 'My job nowadays is to go and print what better men say. I sometimes think I've never really done anything worth while for our cause.'

'Don't be silly. Isn't it anything to have given your whole life to it?'

'I dunno . . .' Thomas began : but stopped.

Mabel started up.

There was a loud knock at the street door. They heard it pushed open, and the tread of two or three men in the passage.

'They're coming up here,' said Thomas. 'Hardy said he might come round.'

There was a loud knock at the door.

'Come in,' said Thomas. He went to the door and opened it.

When he did so a police constable stepped into the room : behind him a plain clothes detective.

They stared at Thomas for a moment, seeming to dwarf him by their height and heavy bulk.

'Well,' said Thomas, after a bit, 'any trouble?'

The detective stepped forward.

'There's no need for me to ask if you're Thomas Devlin,' he said, 'because I know you by sight.'

'Yes, I'm Thomas Devlin.'

'I'm afraid, Mr. Devlin, I've got a warrant here for your arrest—and a search warrant, too.'

'What for? I'm an honest man. There must be some mistake.'

'No mistake,' said the detective. 'You work a small hand press down in the basement here. Whoever's at the back of you, the imprint's yours.'

Thomas nodded.

'And you've been issuing a lot of very foolish pamphlets lately. There's one of my men downstairs just found a pile of these Invergordon leaflets—with your imprint on them. I've got to arrest you under the new Act. There's the warrant.'

There was a pause.

'Well,' said Thomas, 'do you want me to come with you now?'

'Yes,' said the detective.

'Can't you give me time to make a few arrangements first?'

'I must ask you to come at once, please. We don't want a crowd of people round here. And I must search this room before we go, too. I'm under orders to confiscate all the printed matter I find here.'

Mabel opened the cupboard door and showed the stores of pamphlets. In a surprisingly short time they had searched the room and made a clean sweep.

Thomas began to make rapid arrangements with Mabel.

'We're going to the Central Police Station,' he said. 'Will you tell them what's happened at the paper at once? Go and see them yourself. Then come along and we'll see what we can arrange about bail.'

'I wouldn't count on bail, Mr. Devlin,' said the detective. 'The authorities at headquarters aren't playing. I'm afraid this is a serious business for you.'

'I'll come, anyhow,' said Mabel.

Before going, Thomas kissed her and held her in his arms.

'It'll be all right,' he said.

'Good-bye,' said Mabel. 'I'll be along directly.'

The door closed : and she was alone.

She stood silent for a long time, thinking and seeing nothing.

Then she slowly walked to the window and pulled the curtains. How grimy they were. Then she sat down beside the table which still carried the remains of tea. Many pictures of her broken and tattered life passed before her. She saw her hopes of the future torn in ragged dirty pieces, fluttering away. She knew now that she would never have a home : that from now on she need never hope for a home. The pictures of the little house she had begun to see changed to pictures of rooms in worse and worse streets : to fierce poverty, bare boards, and fireless grates, to comfortless old age.

Yet she felt calm and almost joyful. She had seen the look in Thomas's eyes. She knew he was living through the proudest and happiest moments of his whole life. She fell to thinking of the red and white cheeks, the wild black hair, he used to have. And gradually her heart grew light.

For a long time she sat silent and still until the penny in the gas was used up and the fire flickered out into cold, lifeless grey. Then she rose and put on her mackintosh to go out again. It was still wet from the afternoon's rain.

BUSTING HIM ONE

Zed was the very chap for the game and he caught on as soon as Arthur mentioned it : not that it was a put-up job.

Zachariah his real name was : Zachariah Claydon. His old dad worked up in the Potteries, where they went in for religion in those days : and they called him Zachariah, because the Bible said the Lord was displeased with Zachariah's father ; or for some such reason. They always were a funny lot in the Potteries.

The other kids found Zachariah too much of a mouthful, so they called him Zak or Zed : but Zed was the name that stuck. He always was a fast worker—and handy with his fists.

Arthur and Zed were walking to work. It was a wonderful morning, and Arthur sighed. The morning made him feel glad, but it made him feel sorry too. The light and freshness of the air made him feel glad he was alive : then the work looked like a bad dream, and he could hardly believe it was real.

'Gawd's truth,' he said to Zed, 'what a day! Air like champagne—only it's free. And what a factory, fancy having to go and spend the day in there.'

Zed nodded.

'That chap Boulder,' said Arthur, 'is a bloody swine. I can't make out how they get like that. I can't make out how they always get hold of chaps like that for works managers. Where do they dig them up?'

'It's human nature,' said Zed. 'Some like bullying. That's all it is. There's always some likes bullying other people. Look at the kids playing in the street.'

'I suppose you're right,' said Arthur, 'only we ain't kids: not by a long chalk. We're grown men with wives and kids of our own. We ought to be able to combine together against bullies. Why the hell can't we?'

'You never will now,' said Zed. 'Since the General Strike things have been worse than ever. Don't you see what a clever idea this making of a permanent unemployed class of two million is? It's just to cut the bloody hamstrings of those that are in work.'

'Do you mean you think it's been done on purpose?'

'I don't say it was done on purpose in the first instance,' said Zed. 'These things happen. But see for yourself the use that's been made of it these last ten years. It's the same in every factory nowadays. They press and squeeze further every week, and you can do nothing but squeal. You can't help yourself. That's why the bosses want to keep those two million unemployed.'

They came to the works, where the steady stream of men, women, and boys were pouring in through the red brick pillars and iron gates. The factory wall fell across the sunlight with a cold blue morning shadow. There was still some time to spare, and Zed and Arthur went on talking together in low voices. The gatekeeper eyed them from his little wooden hut.

'First it's the travelling line,' said Arthur, 'then it's Bedaux. They're always up to something to make your job worse.'

His voice grew angrier.

'No sitting down is Boulder's latest little wheeze. There's a good many of those packing machines in my room, and others, too, where the machine minders can take an easy on the end of a packing-case and still be on their job. But he won't ever let the girls sit down. He had one of them in tears over it yesterday. Surely to cripes we're meant to sit down, aren't we, or we wouldn't have been given bums to sit on?'

Zed laughed.

'It's a bit too thick,' said Arthur. 'By God, it would do me good to bust him one in the face, or even to see him busted.'

'Perhaps it may happen,' said Zed. He grinned, showing his white teeth, and held up a square, brown fist in the air, as hard as a piece of teak. 'So long, Arthur,' he said, 'see you dinner time.'

There was trouble from the start that morning. When Arthur reached the packing rooms, he found silence in place of the usual roar and rattle of the shafting. There was trouble in the central plant and no power coming through to the whole of his layout. He found the electricians had been on the job all night.

The sunlight came pouring in through the windows, making pools of light on the pitted concrete floor. The girls and men stood about in their overalls talking in quiet voices. From time to time a boy went by with a trolley load of castings or scrap, which rattled and echoed through the empty machine shops.

Arthur looked about. Somewhere he could hear Boulder's voice—talking loudly and angrily. Boulder was always talking. He was telling the packing machine girls to get to their places in the line and not to idle about, even though their machines weren't running.

'What the hell——?' thought Arthur.

Arthur was a maintenance engineer. He had a lathe in almost constant use, remaking, re-turning, regrinding, re-edging a number of the cutting and punching tools which shaped and stamped the tins as they went through. There were dozens of different patterns, and several sizes were needed on each machine, according to the thickness of the material and variations in speed and exact effect that was needed. This part of his work was highly skilled, and he had to know all the machines and all their tricks and habits backwards. It was his extra grasp of the complete work that all the machines in his shop were handling that had got him out of the line five years before: just as somewhere in an orchestra there's one man who knows the whole score well enough to conduct a performance.

At length, quarter of an hour late, the power came through: the shafting rattled briskly into action, and one by one the machines came to life, each moaning, roaring, or crashing with its own note. At once the whole wing which had seemed empty before was filled with uproar of noise, and every man and girl was caught up in the roaring flood, hands and eyes riveted to the machine on which they were working.

After production had been in full swing for twenty minutes, one of the machines in Arthur's layout jammed with a sudden crash. He ran to it and saw at once what had happened. A worn eccentric drive and cam had allowed one of the movements to fall a fraction behind the cycle of the machine. The travelling line of metal containers became gradually late, until the die-stamp that was supposed to fall inside the containers began catching them on the edge and smashing them out flat. In a few moments the machine was jammed by chewed-up metal.

The girl of nineteen who was minding the machine began to clear the twisted metal away. Arthur gave her arm a slap.

'Take it away,' he said, 'she's not disconnected yet. Suppose she starts off again. What'll your mother say to me, if I take you home without a hand.'

The girl laughed and rubbed her slapped arm.

'Some of you girls!' said Arthur. 'You'll turn my hair grey.'

He disconnected the power from the machine.

'I ought to put a new rod and cam in here,' he said. 'I could do it in ten minutes.'

As he spoke he found the works manager bending over him. Boulder was talking even before he turned round.

'Too many needless stoppages,' Boulder was saying. 'What the hell are you supposed to do but keep these machines running? Why don't you start up again instead of hanging about?'

Arthur pointed out the trouble.

'She'd only be jamming again,' he said.

'Why didn't you get that seen to last night?'

'I had two men on their machines working overtime two nights ago,' said Arthur. 'I can't keep them every night.'

'Oh,' said Boulder, 'there are plenty of men about this town who'll work without clock-watching. If that's the trouble we'll sack a few.'

Arthur felt a stifled rage. He began to clench his fists automatically. Boulder had introduced a costing system, by which overtime could only be charged against tonnage actually produced. On the books work on the machines out of hours did not exist. It only existed in default.

Arthur's anger nearly overcame him. He saw the faces and eyes of the other men turned towards him with sullen curiosity. One day Boulder would get it. Arthur or one of the other men would bust him.

'Get her started up,' said Boulder. 'And if the tins don't follow close enough make the girl keep them closed up with her hand. That's what she's there for.'

Arthur started the machine up and stared at its racing pinions and arms, at its whirling central movement and its eccentric cross movements, and the regular thudding of the die-stamp. His anger left him feeling slightly weak.

'Look here, my girl,' he said, 'you'd better not keep the containers closed up with your hand. It isn't safe. I can't help what he says. This machine's going to do funny things to-day.'

Arthur was quite right. In another twenty minutes the machine jammed again with a sudden rending shock. The spinning leather belt went looping and curling round the overhead shafting and became entangled with the belt of the next machine.

There were loud shouts and running feet. In a moment the power was disconnected from the central shafting, and the machines died away into silence, with twenty different groans. The men and girls stood back from their places and looked at each other.

Arthur saw that the worn rod and cam that had caused the trouble in the first place were now twisted completely out of shape. It was a matter of some pride to Arthur that he could produce a new part from his store ready made.

The whole line was now thrown out of work for ten minutes while his spare part was fitted. Boulder abused Arthur as he was working: rated and threatened him as a schoolmaster threatens a small boy.

Once more the other men looked on in sullen silence. They shared Arthur's feelings. The same hatred was working behind each face; there wasn't a man there, from the boys of nineteen and twenty to the grey-headed impassive fathers of families, who was not aching to give Boulder a good thrashing, who would not have gladly given a week's wages to have plugged an iron-hard fist into his pudgy face.

When the machines were started up again Boulder still stayed in the packing-room. They had lost twenty minutes on production time since the morning had begun. He stood behind each machine in turn, finding fault with the men working on it.

At the far end of the line was a machine recently imported from the Continent, known as the Kreder Vertical. It took the place of four previous machines, doing the work of the four faster and better, and taking up less space even than one of them. It twisted the paper covers for the wrapping. It divided them into four strips, each printed in four colours, and fed them to the packing machines at a sufficient speed to keep pace with the line of travelling containers. The working parts of the Kreder upright travelled more quickly than the eye could follow and it had improved production speed by four per cent.

As Boulder passed down the forest of rattling machines he saw a man sitting on a packing-case beside the Kreder Vertical: he was watching it intently and occasionally put his hand out to make an adjustment to a control while the machine was running.

'Get up!' Boulder began shouting to him: but his voice was lost in the roar, and the man made no move. Others near him turned to look at him, and back at Boulder.

'That man sitting by the Kreder, get up!' yelled Boulder. Arthur from the end of the line glanced up and saw that something was happening. He saw that the man by the Kreder was Zed. He stepped away from his lathe and began to walk towards the Kreder.

'Come on,' said Boulder to Zed, 'up you get. I've said often enough I'm not going to have this lounging about at the machines. You can't work sitting down.'

Zed turned round without getting up and looked at him for a long moment.

'Nuts to you,' he shouted above the roar of the machines. Everybody at the nearby machines was staring. Arthur stood close by, and something inside him began to laugh.

'Stand up,' shouted Boulder, 'and get out of here.'

Zed made no movement.

'You're sacked,' yelled Boulder at him. 'Get out of here at once.'

'Sacked be damned,' said Zed.

For a moment they stared at each other, the machines roaring round them. Then Boulder caught hold of Zed by the shoulders and dragged him off the box.

'Now then,' said Zed, 'hands off, if you please.'

Zed tried to shake him off, and Boulder tried to hustle Zed down the aisle between the machines. Every face was turned towards them, watching them through the machines, round the machines, over the top of the machines.

Zed shook Boulder off, and gave him a light tap on the chest that sent him walking backwards off his balance. Then quick as thought Zed brought his right across and smashed it into Boulder's face with all the strength in him. Zed's fist was big and solid and hard as weathered teak. He weighed twelve and a half stone, all bone and muscle, and he knew how to hit.

Boulder went spinning back, crashed into the safety fencing round one of the machines, and went right over inside it. There was a loud yell of alarm from a dozen men. Zed was hauling him back almost before he had landed. The power was shut off. The machines stopped with their various dying noises and a silence fell.

Zed helped Boulder to his feet. He was unhurt except that he was bleeding freely from the mouth where Zed's fist had cut his lip and loosened a couple of teeth : but for a second he had been within an inch of being killed or horribly maimed in the machines.

The men and girls left their machines and stood round looking at him. He was pale green and his legs were trembling.

Zed held him by the arm.

'You can't sack me,' said Zed. 'I'm not employed by you. I'm sent in by the Kreder Company to give that new machine servicing. And I can sit down to my work without your leave.'

Boulder spoke thickly and uncertainly through his torn lip.

'I'll get you sacked for this. I'll have you up for assault.'

'No fear,' said Zed. 'You started on me first. Here are my witnesses. Forty of them.'

'Forty of them,' he said again, and the crowd round them pressed a bit closer.

Boulder looked at them and began to speak. Someone began to boo : and suddenly the whole gang of them were booing and cat-calling till the noise rang and echoed through the empty shops ; then with the boos remarks were shouted.

'Wipe him again, Zed !' said a voice.

'Pity he wasn't minced up,' shouted someone else. The remarks became filthy and obscene. They pressed round Boulder closer and closer, booing and yelling like a set of savages, every man giving way to his pent-up hatred and contempt of

Boulder and of the whole firm. They attacked him with brutal indecencies and with threats of wild savage punishments.

Suddenly they stopped: and acting by one common impulse that arose from the strength of their feeling they walked out of the machine rooms, out of the factory, and back to their own homes for the rest of the day.

Boulder stood alone among the silent mountainous machines. They had frightened him badly. There was nothing he could do.

THE STOKER

Mr. Carstock, who ran the public-house, liked to tell his friends that he was a man without illusions. It was common sense and a strong grasp of practical tangible affairs that he would have you especially recognize and admire in him.

'A pint pot'll hold a pint o' liquor and no more,' was one of his maxims, if he thought anyone was straining a point or wandering from the road of actuality. And by the same symbol he would strive to convey some rather vaguely formulated ideas that life was a matter of working and sleeping, enjoying and enduring, and then returning to the dust: and that to worry your head over anything more abstruse was to try and extract more than the pint from the pot.

Being so sure of this, he could observe absolutely without reflection as he sprawled over his bar. He could watch through the pleasant haze of smoke and the soothing babel of voices, and to him each man was no more nor less elusive than a pint pot.

Tom Farleigh, then, was just the same as his youth had given promise. A strapping lad, Tom: back from three years at sea—stoking, that's what they called the game, brawnier than ever. That blue jersey with its rough roll of collar showed up

Tom's bulk, a good solid fourteen stone: you'd like to see him stripped.

Even Mr. Carstock's unimaginative mind had some picture of Tom, huge and glistening and ferocious, with rivers of sweat channelling down the coal-dust on his back.

No wonder the other men had come in to-night to give Tom a send-off; even that scrawny little bit of sorrel who never came near the place, except for bottled beer on Sunday—Cecil Lough; and, my God! what a name. He could never think of that Cecil, without laughing.

It was just the same as ten years before, when all this lot had been boys together: it was Tom Farleigh this and Tom Farleigh the other, and those boys had to kow-tow to him, whether they liked it or not. Here they were, at it again.

'Your turn, Joe,' shouted Tom, giving the order himself. 'Make it another six bitters, Mr. Carstock; that's the stuff to give 'em.

'Girls?' Tom was saying. 'Girls? I should say so. I could tell you.'

Everyone waited for him to go on.

'Oh, I could tell you,' he said. 'Those mulattoes. I should say they *were* mulattoes.'

Roars of laughter came from everyone.

'You always was one for the women,' a voice suggested.

'Oh, I could tell you a lot now,' Tom went on, looking round as they hung on his words.

'Remember that Sue Parkinson, though? But

I tell you what,' said Tom. 'There's someone 'ere as don't hold with such goings on. 'E'll go and tell the bloody parson as I'm rude.'

Heavy and suety laughter rolled again round the clogged atmosphere.

Everyone laughed except Mr. Carstock, who seldom saw cause to be amused. But his impassive gaze followed the other jeering faces towards the target of the joke. That boy Tom was a bit of a bully. Mr. Carstock had observed, in the past, that he gave young Lough hell's own time. Not his affair, though.

'That's right,' said Lough, as soon as he had a chance of being heard. 'I'm taking down every word you say, Tom: and it's my turn for a round, I think.'

'Well, make mine a double one, see?'

'Go on, Tom,' someone begged. 'You was tellin' us——'

'Well, I *could* tell you,' said Tom. 'I could make you *hungry*. But are you sure I ain't shocking you, Mr. Lough?'

'That's all right, ol' man,' said Lough. 'I'm—I'm married now.'

Tom laughed, all alone, in a high falsetto. Mr. Carstock's detachment grew more marked.

'Married!' croaked Tom. 'Oh, mother dear! Cissie's married!'

Lough blushed. Slowly and obtrusively he felt the hateful heat creeping upwards.

No one had called him Cissie since Tom had

left the village. If only he had not come; he was a fish out of water. He might have guessed Farleigh was the same swine he always had been.

And it was a bit thick: they weren't kids now. No good getting annoyed, though—but he'd damn well answer up.

'Yes, I *am* married,' he said. 'Why not? I happen to be able to support a family.'

'Here's to marriage!'

Lough drank and one or two others did, but Tom stared at them in rebuking scorn.

'Well, I'll be ——,' he said. 'That's one toast I never will booze to. Marriage—the same dish o' cold mutton every blurry night.' He waited and insisted on their obedient laughter. 'Not like. That's what Cissie likes. The sa'—hic—colmurron.'

Lough stood up.

'All right, Tom,' he said, 'sorry we don't agree. Well, I must be off. Have another one, Tom.'

'There you are,' said Tom. 'He's got to go home to bed or his missus'll give him a caning. That's it, mates, eh?'

Mr. Carstock's impassive sight recorded that Lough laughed with the others. At the first possible moment, however, he made his voice heard.

'Well, good-bye, Tom, good luck.' He offered his hand awkwardly.

'Good-bye, Cis—you want to grow a bit fatter. Come off the mutton. Look 'ere.' He compared their two forearms as he shook hands.

'Well, cheero, Tom,' said Lough again. Pulling the door to behind him Lough passed abruptly out of Mr. Carstock's range of observation.

He plunged thankfully into the darkness. Why the hell had he let himself in for this? What humiliation! He shouted out a stream of bad language. It was as if he was expelling all the coarseness from himself—getting rid of it before he got home. To think that his marriage, his home, should have been dragged into this sort of talk. He hit out at the darkness.

'I'm not so bloody strait-laced,' he said out loud, 'but ordinary decency—my God, he's low: he's a brute!'

'He's no conception: he's got no further than being a schoolboy. I've got a better place in the world than he has: he's got no idea what work like mine means. If only I could show him. Yes, I suppose, I meant to show him when I went there to-night. What a hope! He's too thick. But why the hell shouldn't he realize?'

But of these reflections Mr. Carstock, of course, knew nothing, and supposed nothing. He saw that Farleigh had baited Lough; that was the sort of chap he was. The incident was closed as far as he was concerned, when, half an hour later, he pushed the swaying Tom and his friends out into the night.

'You all right, Tom? See you some day. Good night. Good night, ol' man. Good night all. Good night all.'

Mr. Carstock returned to the empty bar and

turned the pint pots up over a bucket, according to his method. Nothing was left in any of them.

Mr. Carstock had noted that Tom was reeling all round the place. But Tom's impression was that the place was reeling all round him. Now the road rose up like a steep hill before his eyes—now it dropped away beneath his feet. At moments the grass bank at the side of the way would suddenly change its position and come between his boots.

The evening swam in one confused composite film shot before his eyes. Laughing faces, the side of the pot, 'Go on, Tom, you're a one, Tom; you don't get no better, Tom; you're the real cheese and no mistake; oh, yes, I'm the Tom; real cheese Tom, I am, and don't you forget it.

'Now how the hell did I come to be leaning up against this gate, thought I was walking along the road?

'My God, yes, girls. I could tell you chaps. But they're gone now. No chaps with you now, ol' man. You'd 'a' made 'em sit up, eh? He's a man that Tom—up to all their games, 'he is. Fine fellow, a man, 'e is.'

Girls, yes, he thought he could do with a girl now, right here. They don't come so frequent, do they, not for all you tell 'em, never when you most want 'em, that's what it is. You set out on the spree deliberate and that seems to take the edge off it like. If there was a girl here now, one with some flesh on her, now, mind you, flesh, that's it, flesh. I'd take her like this and she'd say:

''Oo said you could do that?'

And I'd close 'er mouth now like this, like this. And my hand—

'Oh, Tom!'

He clenched his fist and shut his eyes. A slight groan escaped him.

'Ah, that Sue Parkinson. Dear God, man, wasn't it in this very field—and just such a summer night as this'n? Summer, that was the time for girls; nature's own time.'

The warm and odorous air of the July night inflamed him still further. It was heavy with dim memories; the scent of her in the evening; the sudden gleam in the dark of her skin unsheathed. So sharp was the stab of lust that pierced his body, it brought with it an emotional effect on his intoxicated mind. His heart beat violently—his head throbbed and his eyes filled with tears.

'Poor Tom—all alone now—all alone—longing—longing—oh, hell!'

Something like an ecstasy of anguish passed, leaving a heavy and despondent reaction. He swung away from the gate. His lurching annoyed him now, and troubled him. He was a forlorn, lonely figure, staggering on. And he was feeling sick. His thoughts were no longer mixed: he was feeling sick: he, the fine fellow who could drink the others asleep—feeling foully sick on five pints of swipes, or was it six? What a blasted fool he was not to go home and have his dinner properly.

And he'd upset the old girl, too: she'd have

worried about him. Why hadn't he gone home? He would have come out, and had a few drinks, and gone home to his supper as neat and clean as a whistle, and the old girl would have been as pleased as one o'clock.

'And that was the life, too. Having someone to look after you. Why did he laugh at that Cissie Lough being married? Damn it, you knew you wished you could do as much; that was it, he's stole a march on you. He's doing better than you, for all he's a puny little rat and your talk of mulattoes—foul bitches that they are. And he knows it, too. And, oh God! am I going to spew on that swipes of stuff, honest beer never made a man feel like this: not drunk, just sick.

'But what girl 'ud want to marry you? All you can do is to shovel coal into a furnace away at sea most of the time. Besides, what 'ave you ever got to say to the marrying sort? They want a little rat, not a man, it's not fair though. Oh! I do feel sick.

'Gone to my legs now, it has: if only I could keep walking straight without these jolts, it's enough to make a man sick. What's the matter with me, though? I can't be drunk on that, it's the empty stomach that does it. If only I could get it up I'd feel better then. Come on now, get yourself home. You'll be all right. What'll the old girl be doing? Will she 'ave sat up for me? I suppose she will. I 'ope to God she'll 'ave gone to bed, especially if you're going to be sick.

'Hold up now, Tom: do you remember the first

time you was aboard, staggering about like this, and feeling like this ; it was like this though. Shut your eyes and you might be there. And you got to go back to it to-morrow. He's got the laugh of you, your little spree's over, my lad. Oh, hell, it ain't fair though that bloody little worm of a Cissie should have everything : he can stay on shore and have his girl, and he's no such worm, neither ; you can't do it, that's what it is. Wonder if I sat down for a bit would I feel better ?

'I'd almost sooner have a pain than this : it's enough to get a man down. Oh, hell, why can't I have some o' the things. A man oughtn't to feel as sick as this—like a fist screwing up your guts or summat.'

As Tom lurched home through the dusk, the nausea gradually overcame all the other thoughts and feelings. His memory of the dark country road that he had travelled often as a boy triumphed all unconsciously over the drugged fuddlement of his mind. His steps brought him to the white gate, that glowed softly in the summer darkness, led him round the flagged path past the front door ; his feet rather than his brain knew the front door would be locked and the back door left on the latch for him.

Unaware almost of how he arrived there he found himself sitting on the low horsehair sofa in the cottage room staring at his legs, which were thrust stiffly out in front of him. The strain on the back of his knees aroused him gradually to realize that he had arrived.

He looked round. Well, the old girl had cleared off to bed. That was a comfort. There'd be no asking questions, whether he'd had a good time and that, as much as to say, 'Tom, why didn't you come home? Tom, I've been waiting, waiting; I did think you'd spend the last night with me, Tom. Tom?'

'Well, so he did mean, only those chaps at the pub there, and why should she worry over him so, he was all right. A man liked to go with men; that was only natural he should say good-bye to his friends. She saw plenty of him mornings—and he'd helped in the garden, hadn't he?

'He'd done his best, hadn't he? She didn't expect him to bring home money, did she? It was little enough time a chap got ashore; what the hell fun was there in life if you couldn't enjoy yourself a bit, then? Am I going to be sick, I wonder? Praise God, she is tucked up safe in bed and not waiting up to see you come in, bloody drunk.'

He fell into a profound stupefied silence, abstracting himself from all signs and feelings of life in an endeavour to escape from his nausea.

But he was violently startled out of it by hearing the floorboards creak overhead and then the wire mattress make a 'ping' familiar from earliest years as his mother got into bed.

'Blast her, then! She *had* been waiting up for him to come in, then: waiting upstairs with the light out, so that he shouldn't know. Why should he be nagged at with her waiting up for him; oh!

he hated to think of the old girl sitting up there alone in the dark waiting to hear him come in, and not liking to let him know it. Oh, blast and hell, why should she make herself unhappy on his account? He didn't want her to, he only wanted to make her happy, and acted for it. If she wanted to wait up for him, why wouldn't she do it down in the sitting-room? It was only reasonable, that. And when the hell had he ever told her he didn't want to be waited up for? She oughtn't to have done that, it put him in the wrong.'

His eye now wandered round the room, and the table she had left invitingly spread for him put him further in the wrong. And the food placed carefully in the grate balanced on a wooden log to keep it hot, that put him in the wrong, too. And the kettle left puffing away on the trivet put him in the wrong, and most of all the thick tumbler standing on the table with a double dose of whisky in it. She must have been round to the pub herself and got that for him, and he'd never come in to take it. Oh, hell!

Tom took the food from the fire and looked at it. He felt too sick to touch it now. He would have liked to have eaten it just to thank her, but he could tell her he'd had some up at the pub. But that whisky: she'd got that for him, and she'd like to think he'd drunk it; besides, it might just settle his stomach.

He picked up the kettle and poured a good deal of warm water on the floor and a few drops into the glass. He sniffed at the tepid draught and swallowed it in one shuddering gulp.

Instantly he knew he was going to be sick. He dropped the glass, knocked over a chair, flung open the back door with enough violence to crash it against the picture-studded wall, and rushed into the garden.

In a few minutes he came back feeling very much happier; a load had been lifted from his spirits as well as his stomach. Well, that's over, now we can get along to bed and sleep it off. He looked round the room and laughed. What a hurry he'd been in, quite comic, wasn't it? 'You'd better pick up that chair against she sees it in the morning. Ooopsee—that's it; you are shaky, though, ol' man, get along to bed now: and go up softly so as she won't hear you, she's likely gone off to sleep. Well, her troubles are over for the day and yours, too; you got to go back to your job to-morrer, though, blast it!'

He crept up the stairs; but she was not asleep: she had heard everything, and it was more than she could endure in silence any longer. She must speak to him.

As Tom fumbled about the sitting-room her door opened a crack, and she called:

'Tom?'

'Wot?'

'You're all right?'

'All right? Woddyer mean, all right?'

'I only wanted to know.'

Why couldn't she have gone to sleep, thought Tom ; can't she let it alone and go to sleep?

'Are you coming up to bed now?'

'Give us 'arf a minute.'

'I think I'd come to bed now.'

'Well, you go to sleep, I'm just coming.'

She shut the door and Tom heard her get back to bed. Why the hell should he go to bed before he wanted? He'd got to go back to his ship, to-morrow, couldn't he do what he wanted, for a bit?

However, he stumbled up the stairs, and without undressing flung himself on the bed. He felt precious shaky, and he'd undress in a minute. Just think what it meant, though, back to that bleeding game to-morrow ; no sooner off than at it again.

Why couldn't he stay at home and lead a decent life, though? He couldn't be going to be sick again, could he? He closed his eyes and lay quite still. Preternaturally still.

The bed ploughed on and on in the darkness. It rose and fell in long swoops like a ship. He flung a hand to his forehead to steady his head. He groaned. Suddenly he was asleep.

Tom took his large, red, sullen face in his hands and supported his head with a gesture of hopelessness on the kitchen table. Would the old girl see it?

She peered round at him from the stove.

'Come along, dear,' she said briskly, 'your breakfast'll get all cold.'

'I don't seem to feel I've got the 'eart for it,' said Tom dejectedly.

'Go along now, you naughty boy,' she said. 'Don't let me hear another word; eat it up.'

Tom glanced at it: the eggs were still sizzling and the fried ham was cut in thick, browned slices. He had had no supper the night before: he felt empty. 'Yes,' he thought, 'I want it.'

He chewed slowly, and his mother, peering again over her shoulder at him, saw that his mind was not on the enjoyment of his food as it ought to have been. He caught her anxious glance, but she shot it past his head and pretended she had been scanning the morning.

'Going to rain, eh?'

'I dunno,' said Tom, 'and I doan care.'

A weight of grey and dreary clouds rolled across the sky and across his mind. He felt hopeless. Let it rain.

What did it matter to him, cooped up in the bowels of a stinking machine for weeks on end? What difference whether it was wet or fine, if he never saw the sun? What difference to him if there never was a sun? It wasn't fair: it wasn't a life at all. Work, rotten grub, sleep, work like hell, rotten grub, sleep. Why should he have to live like that? It fair broke a man, that, it got you down.

'Oh, Gawd!' sighed Tom hopelessly.

Why couldn't the old girl say something! Couldn't she see how he was feeling?

He sighed again and bent down to lace up his boots.

'You mustn't be so down, dear,' she said, 'just because your holiday is over. We've all got to work.'

'You don't know,' he broke out, 'you don't know wot it is. It's easy to talk : it isn't a life at all : it isn't fair. I can't stick it.'

Tom found she had come quite close to him ; as he bent down he found her hand on his head. She had taken the chair near him.

'Is it so very bad?' she said.

'It fair breaks my 'eart,' he moaned. 'It breaks my 'eart. You got no idea. Never seein' the sun from day in to day out ; working till your back's broke. We never get up on deck. It isn't fair, it isn't a man's life at all. I tell you I can't stick it. I can't go back. I can't, mother. Why can't I get something decent to do?'

He never noticed in the excitement of his outburst that somehow she had put his head on her knee. He was kneeling on the floor before her chair, his lump of a head resting on her lap. She gently stroked his hair.

'Poor boy,' she said, 'you mustn't worry over it so. You mustn't.'

'Last voyage,' he went on in a calmer voice, 'I kept a calendar in my bunk. I marked all the days as I got on deck and saw the air. Four it was, the 'ole voyage. Four. It ain't right. A man oughtn't to live like that.'

'You'll be back 'ere again in no time,' his mother said.

'Sometimes,' said Tom, 'I feel I could chuck the 'ole thing : wot's the use of being alive? It ain't worth it.'

His mother was silent for a long time.

'You've been thinking, dear,' she said, 'that's the trouble. Where'ud I be if I was always thinking, and worrying?'

'I shall 'ave to start in a minute,' said Tom. 'Can't I not go?'

'Of course you must go. You've signed on for the trip. But I'll tell you what, Tom. Why don't you try and get a job in the docks at Avonmouth? Make inquiries afore you go on board.'

'I 'ave done.'

'Well, I will, too. There's Mr. Carstock's brother's got a good job in some big warehouse there. Likely he'd know of something. We'll find you something in time, Tom. But we've all got to begin at the bottom. Jobs need waiting for, but you've got to go on with what you've got. It's no good giving up.'

'No.'

'You'll promise me you'll go aboard like you've signed on to?'

'Yes.'

'That's right,' she said more cheerfully.

Tom raised his head and got up. He felt a bit better now.

'Talking of jobs,' he said. 'What's that Cissie Lough doing? He's married and all that.'

'Well, he's got his own special line, you see.'

'Wot?'

'Well, carpentering and that; he took up with carpentering first, and then he got employed by a firm of decorators. It's for hand-carving?'

'Wot 'and-carving?'

'Well, in woodwork; Mrs. Parkinson—that's Sue's mother—is caretaker up at Mr. Newall's. She showed me some woodwork he'd done in the dining-room. Wonderful it was, all leaves and fruit, done in wood—like real.'

'Wot does 'e get paid?'

'Well, I 'eard someone say he could get as much as five and six pounds a week when the work was there.'

Tom scratched his head and thought. 'Wosser time?'

'It's on the half-hour. You'd better be starting, it's a good hour's walk.'

Ten minutes later he was striding up the road. It was a chilly morning for summer. He was cold and unhappy. He was rather humiliated: his mother had soothed him, comforted him, put some of the fight back into him. But he felt his manhood had suffered: she had soothed him like a little boy, just as she used to years ago.

That was what he felt: childish. Miserable like a child, unable to battle with the world and make it give him the things he wanted. He could only turn to his old mother and play the whining child. He was no good. What use were his muscles, his swank, the other men flattering? He was only a helpless, crying child. Oh, hell! And to think of those weeks and weeks in the ship. He was beaten, that was it, beaten. The guts were gone out of him. He was up against it; the world was too strong for him. He'd never get his girl and his home and all the things a man ought to have. That was what made a man a man, surely. Living a man's life completely. Not shovelling coals into a furnace—with nothing in life but work and sleep.

Why, Lough was more of a man that he was: he'd got his home and his things round: he could do something. Pretty fool he'd made of himself poking fun at Lough last night. Lough had the laugh of him all the time. How he must have sneered up his sleeve.

Tom was so engrossed in these thoughts he never saw a figure approaching. It was Lough stepping it out briskly to his morning's work.

Lough had caught sight of Tom, and he was dreading the encounter. What beastly thing was he going to say this time? He felt like a child with that sort of man. Farleigh put him in the position of a snivelling little boy again, told him to his face he was a nincompoop, laughed at his thin wrists. Farleigh despised him; thought he was only half a man.

Last night in the pub he had sat it out, and pretended it was all a joke, but he felt humiliated and beaten. He felt that the world was too strong for him. These were things he would not stand up against. They were all symbolized in Farleigh.

Lough felt ridiculously nervous as he drew near. Suddenly Tom looked up and saw him.

'Morning, Tom,' said Lough.

''Ullo, Cissie,' said Tom. Jealousy swept over him, and his own dissatisfaction was sharpened acutely : instantly a sneer came into his voice.

'Off to his little woodcarving,' he said, 'do it pretty, mind !' He wasn't going to be laughed at.

'That's it,' shouted the discomfited Lough genially, 'and you do your stoking pretty, too !'

The shaft went right home : that was it, then, Tom thought : Lough knew that was all he was fit for : back to your shovelling, you damned slave. His cup of misery was full. He trudged gloomily on, brooding on every stride.

Mr. Carstock, who looked out of his window at that moment for a breath of early morning air, noted the meeting. That Tom Farleigh always was a bully, and he had to be cock of his own little walk.

That was the pint in that particular pot.

IF YOU CAN'T BE GOOD, BE CAUTIOUS

An old Lycett lorry came lumberingly into a garage near the Great West Road. This was a ramshackle place with a draughty concrete yard, corrugated iron roofs, and doors hanging by a hinge. It was much used by lorry drivers as a port of call for a chat.

'Hullo, Tom,' said the garage hand to the driver of the lorry. 'You haven't been this way lately.'

'Hullo,' said Tom. 'Cheerio, everyone. I'll have six gallons of the usual, please, and perhaps Bessie will give me a cup of tea if I promise her a kiss.'

Presently Tom, sitting in the cab of his lorry and stirring his tea with a pencil, shouted: 'Did you hear about that young fellow who works for our crowd—Bob Curtain? Curt, we all call him. He's been up before the magistrates to-day.'

'No, go on,' said the garage hand. 'What for —speeding?'

'I don't know,' said Tom. 'It wasn't anything to do with driving. He's a bit of a lad.'

At that moment a second Lycett lorry swung into the filling station, rather too fast, scattering a heap of gravel and a couple of buckets. It pulled up with a jerk, almost striking the tailboard of Tom's lorry. It was Curt.

'Hullo, young fellow,' said Tom. 'How did you get on to-day? So they didn't put you in quod?'

Curt got out of his lorry and glared at him without answering. He began to lounge round the yard with his hands in his pockets.

'No,' he said at length. 'Nor are they likely to.'

'Well,' said Tom. 'What was it all about? What was the trouble?'

'Nothing. All a lot of rot. Just those blasted bobbies trying to put me wrong.'

'But what was the charge?' said Tom. 'If it isn't a rude answer. If you don't mind my asking.'

'No, I don't mind,' said Curt. 'Why should I? It was carrying a gun without a licence, if you want to know.'

Tom pushed his cap off his forehead, and shook his head. 'Well, you're a funny one,' said the garage hand. 'What on earth do you want with a gun?'

'No harm in it,' said Curt. 'I'm just interested in fire-arms, that's all.'

'What did the magistrate say?'

'Oh, a lot of stuff. He tried to make the most of it. Anybody'd have thought I'd committed a crime. A lot of talk about getting into bad company. I didn't listen to half of it.'

'Well, it's all right, isn't it?' said Tom. 'He let you off scot free?'

'No, he didn't. I was bound over. I've got to go and report every bloody month.'

'Well, there's no great harm in that.'

'Yes, there is,' said Curt. 'That's just the swine of it. Didn't I tell you I'd got a better job?'

'I do remember something. What was it?'

'It was up in Manchester, that's what it was, driving a taxi for a chap I know. It was a good opening. Now this has mucked everything up. I can't take it.'

Curt went on mouching round the yard with his hands in his pockets. 'Damn fools,' he said. 'Damned swines. I tell you what it is, Tom. Those swines of police: once they've got their hands on you, they mean to get you. They mean to put you wrong. I'd like to get hold of that fool of a magistrate.'

'Well,' said Tom. 'I'm sorry. Still, if you can't be good, be cautious. That's what I always tell my kids. "Be good if you can, and if you can't, be cautious!"'

A silence followed this.

'Sorry,' said Tom self-consciously. 'It ain't often I go chucking these pearls of wisdom round. Where are you for to-night, Curt? Bristol?'

'Taunton,' said Curt. 'I've got a load of petrol—hundreds of gallons. Some muck the boss has got hold of cheap.'

'I'm on that game, too. I've got to go and pick my load up, then I'll be getting along.'

'Right,' said Curt. 'We're meeting at the usual place later on. That fellow Sid's coming.'

'I'll be there,' said Tom. 'Cheer up, you'll be all right.'

Curt nodded. He cranked up his lorry and moved off but, after driving for a few minutes, decided to wait on the Great West Road for Tom to catch him up. He wanted to unburden himself.

It was now the brown dusk of an October twilight. Lights began to gleam in the evening. A brooding silence fell, and was shattered, and fell again as an occasional lorry crashed by on the first stage of a long night journey.

The river's vaporous breath swirled up from Kew, from Gunnersbury, from Brentford. It coiled round the lamps and across the tattered half-made roads and dying fields. Curt shuddered. He felt the raw edge of the mist against his skin. Its looming shapes hung before him, filling his mind with vague fears of the police, of the bosses, and the power they held over his whole life.

Presently he found a man in a mackintosh was looking up into the cab of the lorry, and asking for a lift.

'Get up if you like,' said Curt, rousing himself. 'She's not exactly one of those super luxury coaches, still, she gets along somehow. Where do you want to go to?'

'Oh, west,' said the other.

Curt laughed. 'West?' he said. 'That seems a bit uncertain. I mean, do you want to go to Bath or Cardiff or Salisbury? They're all west from here. Where *are* you aiming for?'

'Where are you going?' said the stranger.

'Oh, me; I'm going down past Bristol; but I'm meeting one or two pals half-way, and we might find something to do.'

He found the stranger staring at him.

'What's the matter?' he said. 'We have to do something to amuse ourselves. A lot of chaps, who drive lorries, don't get home for a week or more together, so we arrange meeting-places on the road.'

'What for?'

'Oh, just for a bit of a talk; you get to feel a bit cut off when you live and sleep on one of these barrows for days together. The married men feel it most, and this night driving, too, it works on you. Of course, the bosses try to stop our meeting, but then they do so many things against the Act all the time, what the hell can they expect?'

'Do they?' said the stranger. 'What sort of things? You mean they keep you on too long hours?'

'Yes, of course I do,' said Curt angrily. 'You aren't on their side, are you? Because if you are you can get a lift off somebody else, see? I'll pull up right away.'

He began to slow down.

'All right, mate. That's all right,' the stranger said hastily. 'It isn't my trade, you see. I was only asking.'

'Well, I'm telling you. How would you like to drive fifty-seven hours, on a stretch, with only three hours off the whole time? That's what happened to a London man last week. I knew him slightly; the chap lived round Dalston way. Then he crashed, and got killed. At the inquest it came out that he'd been driving for fifty-seven hours without sleep. He leaves a wife and kiddies. He was quite a young chap, not much older than me. How would you like that?'

The stranger made no answer.

'Bit thick isn't it?' said Curt. 'Bit bloody thick, isn't it? By God, it makes me see red. They're all the same, all these bosses. To hell with them! An extra quid's worth more to them than a man's happiness, or a man's life. And the police are simply there to back them up. That's what I say. Throat-cutting would be a damn sight too good for them.'

The stranger still made no answer.

It was now quite dark. They rushed along in that narrow and lonely world that closes round night drivers. They sped through an endless silent tunnel—a cave of darkness. The yellow light of the headlamps flashed on the ribbed walls and roofs to this side and that as deep banks and hedges streamed past. Trees, remote and still, stood for an instant before them, their leaves showing faint and dusty in the light. Then they vanished. The headlamps bored and bored through the darkness of the tunnel. Occasionally a fast-moving car slipped quietly by them.

The stranger watched Curt as his talk ran on and on. He was a young man, twenty-three, or twenty-four at the most. He was good looking, unshaved, unwashed, with black, oily smears on his forehead and face. His hair flew in the wind, and he lounged at ease behind his wheel, driving the lorry with reckless speed and skill. He talked ceaselessly, seeming to keep only half his attention on the yellow rings of light, and the wall of darkness ahead.

They scraped a corner, two wheels mounting a bank and tilting the lorry up at a sharp angle.

'All right, all right,' said Curt. 'Don't get windy. It's this blasted steering. You just ought to feel the back lash. I tighten up the ball joints after every journey. The worm-and-segment's not too good. Takes a bit of getting used to. Of course the boss got her cheap, and he's never spent a penny on repairs yet.'

'How are the brakes?' said the stranger.

'Brakes?' said Curt. 'They're comic. I oughtn't to take her out on the road like this at all, really. The hand brake acts on the back wheel, only it doesn't act. And I don't like using the foot-brake much; it puts too much strain on the rear gearbox bearing.'

'Why don't you drive slower?' said the stranger. 'Be more careful.'

'Hells bells,' said Curt. 'You couldn't drive much slower. Still, I expect you're wise. A pal of mine was telling me to be cautious only to-day. What he said to me was: "If you can't be good, be cautious." Don't you think that's a pretty good way of putting it?'

The stranger said nothing.

'Well,' said Curt, 'I think it is, especially when

the police are such swine. They love to get it in for you.'

'What makes you say that?'

'Because they are,' said Curt angrily.

'I'll tell you what's been happening to me.' And he drew the lorry up at the side of the road and looked intently down the long moonlit stretch in front of him.

'Or perhaps I won't tell you,' he said. 'I'm afraid I'll have to put you off here—I've got to meet some friends of mine.'

As the stranger was getting down, another lorry lumbered by, and Tom leaned out of the cab and waved to Curt.

'Look here,' said Curt, 'We're getting near Savernake. This is all Lord Harleigh's Estate round here; if you care to wait a bit, you'll get another lift. Sorry I can't take you any further.'

'That's all right,' said the other man. 'I shall do fine.'

'So long,' said Curt. 'Good luck, old man.'

He let in his clutch, and with many jolts the transmission took up the load and the lorry started forward. In a mile or two he swung off into a side lane and nosed cautiously along. It was little more than a soft, grassy track. The trees of a thick wood bordered it on each side—their branches scraping and slapping the lorry as it passed. Then his head-lights picked out a dark, bulky shape under the boughs, and he pulled up. As his eyes became accustomed to the clouded moonlight, he saw there were two other lorries waiting for him.

'Hullo,' said Curt. 'Cheerio, Tom. Hullo, Sid. how's things?'

Sid was on the road from Bristol up to London. He had brought a friend with him, a butcher's assistant from Bristol, who wanted a night out. Curt promised to take the butcher back to Bristol by the morning.

'Who was it that you were talking to when I passed?' said Tom.

'Oh, just a chap I'd given a lift to,' said Curt.

'You're a fool to go picking up with people,' said Sid. 'As long as you didn't start blabbing to him——'

'Of course, not,' said Curt. 'What do you take me for? I think I shall turn round right away,' he went on. 'Might as well get it done.'

Sid nodded.

'How's she starting up nowadays?' he asked.

'Not too bad. It takes two of us most mornings. When I swing her alone, it leaves me feeling as if I hadn't the guts left to pull the skin off a rice pudding.'

Tom laughed.

'Blow the top off a glass of beer, you mean,' he said.

'When I'm too weak for that, I'll give you the beer,' said Curt. After a lot of manœuvring he backed his lorry round.

'Aren't you chaps going to turn?' he said, getting down.

'Why?' said Sid. 'Plenty of time later. Are you getting windy?'

Sid was a country chap by birth—yet he looked more of a townee than either of the others. His hair was black, and smoothed back, and he wore a bright-coloured jumper, and a ring on his signet finger.

They spoke all the time in low voices, saying as little as they could. Presently they fell silent.

'Well,' said Curt. 'Shall we start?'

'Might as well,' said Sid. 'Rouse up, Tom.'

'Not me, Sid,' said Tom, who was sitting with his feet up in the cab of his lorry. 'I'm not in this. I've got a wife and two kids at home.'

'Come on,' said Sid. 'It's only a bit of sport.'

'Not me,' said Tom. 'You'd better buck up. It'll be daylight soon.'

Curt left Tom in his lorry, and walked off with the others in the darkness. His heart was beating.

'What's the idea?' he whispered to Sid. 'Same as last time?'

'Yes,' said Sid. 'That, and a bit more. Don't talk. There's the torch; keep by me, I know this place like a book.'

Sid moved so quickly and quietly in the dense darkness under the trees it was hard to keep track of him. Curt could feel the other fellow, the butcher, somewhere close by, though he couldn't see him.

Suddenly Sid crouched down.

'Wait,' he said. He touched Curt's arm. 'Quick, you fool.'

Curt knew what to do. He shone the electric torch full on the branches of the tree about him. In the sudden glare, it seemed that the whole tree was as full of roosting pheasants as a hen house. They showed up black and flustered in the sudden light.

Sid at once fired into the tree point blank with a sawn-off sporting gun. There was an immense crash of noise, which filled the whole night with repeated echoings : wings beat and branches rustled.

Curt felt a touch on his arm.

'I've got two,' said Sid. 'Quick, we'd better move away from here.'

After a little while they stopped and Sid gave Curt the dead birds.

'This is a good place,' said Sid. 'Let's try again.'

'That shooting will bring along every keeper in the place,' said Curt. 'That's enough for one night. I always said it was a damn fool way.'

'Don't get milky,' said Sid. 'Put the light on.'

Another tree was silhouetted : the gun crashed again. They got another bird.

'Christ !' said Sid. 'There's someone coming.' They lay stock still. Curt could feel his heart in the roots of his tongue. The footseps were coming nearer.

A voice called. Sid whispered : 'They're coming this way.'

Suddenly there was a light in the trees, and the voices were right on top of them.

'Run!' said Sid.

Curt found himself at once alone, running over the broken ground in pitch darkness. There were loud shouts and lights just behind, and he hurled the two birds away as he ran. He plunged into brambles, which slashed his face and his clothes.

He fought with the clinging brambles frenziedly, as if they had been hands in the darkness holding him. He felt they nearly had him now. He'd put himself in their hands this time. What was going to happen?

Then he was clear of the brambles and running on open grass skirting the side of the wood. He saw sheep starting up in the darkness across a field. Then he found he was no longer being followed. He lay for a while in the deepest shadow, till the distant voices and movements died right away.

After wandering in the woods for another half-hour, he found his way to the lorries. The others were still missing.

'You're a damn fool,' Tom said, when he told him what had happened. 'Why can't you keep out of this sort of thing for a bit?'

They waited, Curt only anxious now to get away as quickly as possible. Presently they heard voices. The clouds were clearing and the moonlight grew brighter every moment. They saw Sid and the other man coming towards them dragging a heavy burden.

'What the hell——' said Tom.

It was the carcase of a newly killed last season's lamb. Tom took a look at it and went to the handle of his lorry.

'When it comes to sheep-stealing,' he said, 'I'm going.'

'Don't be in such a hurry,' said Sid. 'What d'you think I brought a butcher with me for? You stay and have a joint off it, Tom.'

'Not me,' said Tom.

'Look here,' said Sid to Curt, '*You're* going to take this bloke back to Bristol, aren't you? He knows just where to sell this bit of mutton.'

'I'll get you retail prices for it,' said the butcher.

'Right,' said Sid. 'We'll just sling it on Curt's lorry.'

'All right,' said Curt, watching them, but his heart sank.

'Don't you take it,' said Tom.

'Shut your mouth,' said Sid. 'He'll take it.'

'All right,' said Curt. 'Let's move off. I've had enough for one night.'

'It's easy,' said Sid. 'We'll do it again.' He spoke with perfect assurance.

Curt started up his lorry. But as the engine fired and banged into life in the night silence, they heard the sound of another car. All listened, looking at each other without speaking. 'It's only a car passing in the distance,' Curt thought. But what if it were something else—someone who'd got wind of them? The sound was coming nearer, then he saw headlights flash. In another moment a car bumped slowly into view along the rough lane.

'Christ!' said Sid. 'That's a police car—a Morris.'

Curt leaped into the driving seat of his lorry, raced the engine, and let in the clutch. His was the only one of the three lorries which faced the way of escape : and he had the stolen sheep.

As the car approached his lorry jerked forward. In the glare of his headlights Curt saw the man who had travelled with him, and he could see now that he had plain-clothes-man written all over him.

'The swine,' he said to himself.

In another moment he was clanging up the broken lane. The lorry lurched from one side to the other as he struck deep ruts and pits. He held on to the steering-wheel with all his strength, letting the engine gather power. He could feel the dangerous give of the steering-gear as the front wheels took shock after shock.

After a few minutes of this rough work, he turned out into the main road. He was on a long, straight stretch, dipping and rising in the moonlight. With the accelerator jammed against the footboards he was soon doing fifty down the slopes. Then he saw the headlights of another car rising and dipping behind him. He was being chased. Soon he knew the car behind was coming up quickly. The headlights began to lighten the road all round him. His lorry was making noise enough for a traction engine. He crashed and thundered down the hills. Every bolt in the old Lycett banged and rattled. The wheel kicked violently in his hands, he could hardly hold it. He was only waiting for something to go.

The deep shadows of the trees and banks tumbled by him, writhing as they went; streaming, interlacing, barring his way. The black silhouette of his own lorry hovered beside him. He felt the car drawing nearer: he felt hands closing in on him. Dark fears of punishment, imprisonment, bubbled up from his lowest level. What would they do with him?

He clutched the wheel more firmly. The other car was right on him. A side turning rushed towards him, and he wrenched his lorry round. It struck a bank, swayed at a sickening angle, and then was on the road again. The turning was a narrow lane, climbing steeply.

He heard shouts behind him and knew that the other car had overshot the turning. He raced his engine in low gear, climbing slowly. By the time he had reached the top of the hill he saw the lights coming after him again.

Then he was rushing, thirty, forty, fifty miles an hour again, holding desperately to a narrow dropping road that overhung a deep valley. The road on his near side vanished into sheer emptiness.

The engine began to pop back in the carburettor. Curt knew there was plenty of petrol and he had cleaned the pipes and filters recently. An inlet valve must have burnt out or stuck. He muttered curses to himself.

Then he could see a flame through the floor-boards, where the clutch pedal came through. As he glanced down, it was spreading. He opened the offside door in readiness. He tried the brakes, but they made no difference.

'I shall be dead before they get me,' he thought. 'I shall be dead in five minutes.'

He heard a loud metallic crash against the bottom of the crankcase. At the same instant he found the steering-wheel twisting loosely in his hands. 'The track rod's gone,' he thought. 'That's the end.'

His lorry leapt up the offside bank at fifty miles an hour; it lurched off and rushed at the other edge. Curt tried to jump clear, and saw the clouds and stars beneath his feet. Then the lorry came over on top of him—a huge black hurtling mass . .

At the same instant the Morris car with a dry skid and a scream of brakes drew up in his tracks. Two men flung the door open and began to climb out. For a second or so they watched in silence.

With crash after crash the lorry plunged down into the valley, turning over and over. It came to rest, and instantly a column of red flame rose straight in the darkness as the petrol exploded into fire. Then it turned to smoke and fitful bursts of flame thirty and forty feet high.

'Good God,' said one of the policemen. 'That's the end of him.'

'Young fool, young fool.'

They began to stumble quickly down the hill in the darkness.

Curt watched them vanish. He was lying beside the hedge where he had been thrown as the lorry overturned. He found he was quite unhurt.

As the police officers vanished in the darkness, he began to walk quickly away.

'It was bad luck on Curt,' he began thinking to himself. 'But perhaps he's better dead. I'll be in Manchester to-night. I'll be in Manchester to-night, and start on that new job.

After a few minutes walking and running the flames were hidden by a shoulder of the hill and he slackened his pace.

'I'll get away with it all right,' he whispered. 'I shall always get away with it. Watch me!'

A JOB AT STAEDTLER'S

Maisie's Walter came from Chipperfield. When Dad heard this he at once asked: 'Has he got a job at Staedtler's?'

'No,' said Maisie. 'He's at a furniture-maker's. He's been working there ever since he was a boy.'

'Furniture-making?' said Dad. 'That ought to be fairly safe. People will always want furniture as long as they've got homes. Still, Staedtler's is the place: that's a fine firm to be in. And there's a lot of unemployment over at Chipperfield too.'

Maisie's Walter was a slow-moving fellow, and slow of speech. He was strong, and heavily built. He said very little, but what he said was sensible. He had a very red face and very blue eyes: and, now and again, one or two large lumpy spots appeared on his forehead. Walter was as good a centre-half as you could find anywhere outside League football. The Town team had been much interested in him, and would have signed him on but for his slight deafness.

As soon as Dad met Walter he formed a good opinion of him. Mother liked him, too; but she said: 'Well, I should have chosen a man with a bit more go in him at Maisie's age. Still Walter's Maisie's choice and I am sure he's as good and steady a chap as you would wish. After all she's one of the quiet ones herself. He's kind to children, and he sticks to his job; and when you've said that you've said a lot.'

Maisie and Walter were married on a bright Saturday afternoon in October, and both Mother and Dad showed everybody that they felt a very deep pleasure and satisfaction.

After the service at the church, a large party of people crowded into their little front room. More than once Dad went up to Walter and put his hand on his shoulder. Walter and Maisie stood together in the window and people could see them standing there from the street, through the lace curtains; Maisie still in her white dress, still holding her flowers, and Walter in a new dark blue serge suit, with a stiff collar.

Neither Walter nor Maisie said anything. They stood side by side, and smiled when people congratulated them. Mother bustled about the room, bubbling with excitement, talking to everyone at once, and offering drinks all round.

One of the guests of honour was Mr. Truslove—the old master from Walter's school—a small man neatly dressed in black, with white hair cut very close. He had a long talk with Dad. Before going Mr. Truslove made a short speech, and said that Walter was one of the best boys he had ever known, and Maisie was lucky to have him.

One or two of Maisie's relations remarked to each other, after he had finished speaking, that the luck was not all on one side.

About nine o'clock in the evening, Maisie and

Walter took the train over to Chipperfield; they arrived at their new home, by tram, carrying Maisie's suitcase with them.

They had quite a large room at the top of a house—a corner-house, with a clear view up two streets. Maisie had chosen the room because it seemed bright and airy. Opening out of the bed-sittingroom was their own tiny kitchen. There was a gas stove in the kitchen and a sink out on the landing. They shared a lavatory two floors down with the other people in the house.

When Maisie opened the door and saw her new home finished and ready for the first time, she stood looking round it in silence. 'It's lovely,' she said at last, 'really, it's lovely.'

Walter began to help her off with her coat, and laid it at the foot of the large bed. Maisie took off her new hat, and looked at herself in the glass in the dressing-table, and patted the coils of fair hair over her ears.

'This dressing-table is lovely, too. I never knew you'd make everything as good as this. It's far better than Mum ever had.'

'I've been working at this suite for the whole year,' said Walter. 'I knew you were going to like it, Maisie. That's why I never let you see anything of it before I'd finished it. I wanted to keep it as a surprise.'

Walter had made every piece of the furniture himself. He had bought the wood at cost price through the furniture-makers where he worked.

Their room looked fresh, and clean, and shining. Maisie had chosen a plain wallpaper of cream, unlike the dark brown and red patterned wallpapers in her mother's house; and she had bought for the floor a plain blue linoleum, with a simple green and blue check round the border. Walter's furniture was made from the most expensive mahogany. It stood large and massive, and french-polished gleaming from the walls like dark lustrous mirrors. There was a wardrobe, a chest of drawers, a dressing-table with a mirror, and the double bed.

'It's all seasoned wood,' said Walter, 'and it's as well made as furniture ever was. Our foreman was up here the other day to see it; and he said if we were selling a suite like this through one of the big London shops, people would have to pay seventy or eighty pounds for it.'

Maisie nodded.

The next morning Walter brought Maisie her breakfast in bed on a tray. 'You must have it in bed for a week,' he said. 'You're tired out after all the getting ready for the wedding, and keeping on your work too till the very last.'

'Anyone would think I was Lady Something, lying in bed for breakfast,' said Maisie.

Suddenly she put her arms round him. 'I feel quite frightened,' she said.

'What of?'

'We're too happy; I'm frightened something will happen.'

'In what way?' said Walter.

'You might go and lose your job.'

'That's not likely,' said Walter. 'We're a good firm; been going fifty years. Don't you worry, Maisie. You might as well take it easy now while you can,' he said. 'You may have hard enough work later on.'

'Why?' said Maisie.

'Oh, well,' said Walter. 'There's always hard work for married people. I shall have to work hard at my job; and you'll have to clean up and look after the children.'

'Perhaps we shan't have any children,' said Maisie. 'Plenty of people don't these days,' and she gave a little laugh.

'It's wrong to marry and not have children,' said Walter. 'That's one thing that's quite certain.'

So their married life started.

For the first six months Maisie and Walter were, in their quiet way, wonderfully happy. Sometimes Walter would come home to dinner in the middle of the day: sometimes Maisie would pack up enough for both of them and take it to Walter's factory: and they would eat it alone in the quiet workshop while Walter's mates were out. They decided that they would take it into the nearby square gardens every day in the summer.

Chipperfield is one of a string of several small towns, all joined together. There are no smart streets nor showy shops. All the roads are cobbled; a few red and green trams run through them on a single route; but there is not much traffic of any kind. The town is made up of works and factories with straight streets of small houses round them, in brown, soot-sprinkled ranks—all very much like each other. At the corners are occasional pubs and muddled little grocers' shops.

On most days Maisie used to walk into the old Market Street—the only large shopping street in Chipperfield. There she found a draper's shop with a showy modern front, a blackened town hall, and a statue. Every day she saw hundreds of men standing up and down the street, doing nothing. They were very quiet. Sometimes one or two were speaking together: now and again a newspaper would be passed from hand to hand. For the most part they stood singly and in silence. She often saw old Mr. Truslove talking to one of them: he seemed to know many of them by name. And each man to whom he spoke showed a faint spark of answering life. Walter told her that Mr. Truslove was working every minute of his time in helping to get them jobs: collecting clothes and money for them, and arranging clubs and schemes of work.

All went very well with Maisie and Walter for about six months. Then there was a bombshell.

One warm April evening, Maisie was sitting by the window, sometimes sewing, sometimes just looking into the street, watching the children playing below. The yellow sunlight came slanting in, throwing bright patches on the blue and green oilcloth. Gradually the dusk closed round her and she realized Walter was very late. She stood up and put her sewing away : she walked into the kitchen and lit the gas stove. She stood uncertainly in the dusk, wondering whether to begin putting out the things for supper. Then the door opened and Walter came in. He hung his coat up and greeted her but all the time he kept his face turned away.

'What's the matter, Walter?' she said. 'Something's happened?'

Walter nodded.

'What?'

'It's bad news, Maisie,' he said. 'I never thought it possible.'

'Not your job?' said Maisie.

'Yes,' said Walter. 'I'm losing it.'

Maisie looked at him in silence. She felt her heart beating suddenly in her throat : she felt as if she had suddenly seen a sickening terror threaten her : she looked at Walter unable to speak. After a moment the fear went further off and she began to feel more calm.

'Don't worry,' she said, putting her arms round him. 'It'll be all right, you won't be out of a job long.'

'I wouldn't have thought it possible,' said Walter. 'It's not just *my* job—it's the whole firm; they're shutting up.'

They sat down facing each other across the kitchen table, forgetting all about their meal.

'But I thought they were so sound and safe,' said Maisie.

'So they were. Doing nicely: but now the whole firm's been bought over by some big London people, and the works at Chipperfield are going to be done away with.'

Maisie knitted her brow. 'That's not fair,' she said.

'You see, we're all out of jobs,' he explained. 'The whole of the factory is shutting up: just bought out—everybody's in the same boat.'

'I wish you could get a job in Staedtler's works,' said Maisie. 'That seems safe enough.'

'Ah,' said Walter. 'Everyone wants that. And jobs at Staedtler's are pretty hard to get. They're always safe: you need someone to push you in at Staedtler's. It's no good trying without.'

'Couldn't you get hold of Mr. Truslove to help you, Walter? He thinks so well of you.'

'He might help,' said Walter.

At first Maisie and Walter were very hopeful. Maisie simply could not think of Walter as an unemployed man. She could not connect him with the silent groups that hung about in the old Market Street day after day.

Very early every morning Walter would take out his bag of tools, visit every place on the outskirts of Chipperfield and the neighbouring towns, where he knew there was a bit of building going on, to see if they needed carpenters. He walked a good many miles each day.

Every day, at first, Maisie looked hopefully and questioningly at Walter, when he came in, and he told her where he had been and what had happened. After a week or two his answer was only a shake of the head and a sigh. Soon he had been out of work a month: then three months. The summer grew full and hot. A sweep of blue July sky hung over the grey cobbled streets and sooty box-like houses of Chipperfield. Once or twice Walter and Maisie ate their dinner in the square garden as they had planned during the winter. But behind the sky and the hot asphalt, and the children's shouts, and behind all the long summer months and hours, there was a deadly fear: their own married life with its joyful hopes seemed to have been taken and locked away from them.

In another month or two, by the end of the summer, things began to look really bad. As the winter came on, the work on the new building plots at the outskirts of the town grew less and less. Several of the foremen whom Walter had been visiting regularly turned nasty and told him to keep away.

One morning he said to Maisie: 'I'm not going out to-day, what's the use? My shoes are through. I only wear them out walking round. There's nothing doing: so I might as well stay here.'

'Go on trying,' said Maisie. 'Keep it up till the end of this week.'

Walter sighed, and picked up his bag of tools, which he had been carrying round since the spring. He kissed her and went out. A grey fine rain was drifting over the cobbles. From the window she watched him standing at the gate, and realized that he did not know which way to go. She began to cry, and after he was out of sight would have given anything to have had him back again.

The grey drifting rain went on all day, and he came home soaked and utterly dejected.

'It's no good,' he said. 'They're stopping work everywhere. There's not a chance of a job.'

'It seems so silly,' said Maisie. 'So many people out of work, and yet so many people wanting houses. There's plenty of overcrowding in this town, and families living together in one room: and yet they stop work on building.'

Walter nodded. 'It's lack of the money to build with,' he said. 'And no one's got any money to buy houses when they build them.'

'If only you could get a job at Staedtler's,' said Maisie. 'They never put people off. They even seem to be going in for a larger staff, I've heard. Can't old Mr. Truslove do anything to get you into Staedtler's, Walter?'

They sat silent. Walter's massive furniture made looming shapes of shadow against the walls. It grew very quiet and dark in the room, and after a long time Walter's voice said in the darkness: 'Well, Maisie, it's no good going on thinking things.'

Mr. Truslove was very kind. He promised Walter to do his utmost. And he found Maisie a place as a daily with some people whom he knew:

two miles away right outside the town ; only work-people lived in the town. It was very hard work, keeping her on the go from eight o'clock till eight o'clock with Wednesday afternoon and Sunday free : but it brought in 10*s*. 6*d*. a week.

There was nothing for Walter to do now but to stay at home, tidy up the room, do the washing, and have a meal ready for Maisie when she came back from work. And so the winter months passed —Maisie in work and Walter out.

One evening—it was February now and Walter had been out of work for nearly a year—Mr. Truslove came in to see them. Maisie had just come back from her place. They sat on each side of him leaning forward, and listening intently. Mr. Truslove was white-haired and energetic—he spoke quickly, and gave them a long, rapid account of all he had been doing to find a way of getting Walter into Staedtler's. He had seen the Works Manager, one of the directors, the Staff Controller, and he had even been out to see one of the Mr. Staedtler's in his private house.

'We may work it in time yet,' he said. 'I'm going on trying for you, Walter. They say they only take men into their works on personal recommendation. They like to know about their family records, and just exactly who they are ; its so important to get hold of the right type of man. But I've satisfied the Staff Controller about you, Walter. He's interested in your good record and he says you're just the type they are on the look-out for. I told him your dad was an ex-Army man, too.'

Walter nodded. 'I'm sure I thank you very much, sir,' he said. 'I've been a great trouble to you.'

'Not at all,' said the old schoolmaster. 'I do it because you've always been a sensible steady chap, Walter. You're worth the trouble: and its worth my while trying to get you a place in a firm like Staedtler's.'

Maisie looked from Walter to Mr. Truslove and sighed. 'Isn't there any chance of your being able to do something soon?' she said.

'Well,' said Mr. Truslove. 'I've heard of something that may be useful to Walter right away. There's a big new block of flats going up, out beyond Staedtler's works. Walter ought to go after that at once.'

After he had gone and they were alone together, Maisie said: 'I wish he could do something now, Walter. Do go and get a job at those flats. It seems hopeless to go on like this—I'm so tired.'

She hid her face in her hands and burst out crying. When Walter tried to comfort her she pushed him away and sobbed uncontrollably. Later still sniffing and dabbing her eyes with a rolled-up handkerchief she said: 'Forgive me, Walter. I get so tired and I feel funny. My period's all late: I don't know what's been wrong with me the last week or so.'

Six times Walter went after the new job. At

first they told him they would not be ready for the carpenters and inside fitters for weeks. Another time they told him he had come a day too late, and they had engaged all the men they needed the day before. Again he went and by good luck they wanted to take on an extra man that very day. Walter had his tools with him and started work right away.

Next week he persuaded Maisie to give up her place.

'Our bad times are over now,' he said. 'I felt sure I should get work in time. Now I am in with these people we shall be all right.'

'I'm glad its building you're working on this time,' said Maisie. 'New houses seem needed so badly round here.'

It was at the end of March when Walter began work again. They felt even happier and more excited than they had felt eighteen months before, when they were first married. It was ten shillings a week less than Walter's old job but that scarcely mattered. They took the 'bus into the country on the fine April Sundays, and scented grass and flowers seemed to be springing with fresh hope and life. They sat silent and at peace, filled with contentment and happiness because Walter was at work again. The natural feelings and thoughts of their married life could flow freely once more. Maisie was able to bring flowers home, to take a new interest in their room; to buy a few little things for it—to make plans and think again of the future home, which they would need when they had a family.

After Walter had been in his new job three or four months, Maisie realized that something was going wrong. He came home silent and moody. He never told her anything about his work or the men there. One Saturday evening she watched him, sitting sprawled in his chair, his head sunk on his chest, for twenty minutes or more without moving.

'Buck up,' she said. 'Don't sit moping like that; you're the same every night nowadays. Let's take a walk; or how about the pictures?'

He shook his head.

'Don't feel like the pictures.'

'What is it, Walter?' she said. 'Is it something about your job?'

'No,' said Walter. But after she had asked him a good many times he told her.

'It's hopeless,' he said. 'I've been trying to see the best of it, and not tell you: but I can't go on.'

'What's the trouble?'

'All this cheap work. It's not my style at all, not carpentering as I understand it. They get this machine panelling and screw it up all anyhow: and machine-made moulding glued on by the yard.'

'Well,' said Maisie. 'If that's what they want you to do, I should do it and not worry.'

'I can't help it,' said Walter. 'What's the sense of it? When you've had the training in first-class work I've had all these years, you can't suddenly go and start doing things the wrong way, all shoddy.'

'I should just do what they want.'

'Speed's all they think of,' said Walter. 'They're always round after you, driving you on, and if you're not up to time every minute you're complained of, and you lose your job. When I took that job on, Maisie, there was twelve carpenters working: and now there's only six. They've put off all the others, one by one, because they weren't fast enough, and they're keeping us that are left to do the work of two men each. Then the other chaps, who've lost their work, come calling us blacklegs for taking away their jobs.'

'But it is not your fault,' said Maisie.

'It is in a way,' said Walter. 'But what can I do? I was on from seven this morning till after seven to-night, working full speed the whole time, Maisie and all this week I've been doing what two men was doing last week.'

'It's not fair,' said Maisie. 'They've no right to treat you like that.'

'There's no way out,' said Walter, 'and there's no one to help. They've got you just where they want you; you've got to go exactly their way or lose the job.'

Walter got up and began to walk about the room. She had never heard that anxious ring, almost a tremor, in his voice: she had never seen him so excited.

'And what's the sense of it?' he said almost shouting. 'The work's not well done; it doesn't seem worth doing at all like that—all stuck together anyhow. Everything done cheap and the wood all unseasoned—it'll be breaking up in two or three years time. What's the sense of it? It's all wrong.'

'I'm sorry,' said Maisie. 'Still, it's no good complaining: you're lucky to have any job nowadays. You'll just have to stick it out, Walter. I expect it'll get better if only you stick to it.'

'I'll stick to it,' said Walter, 'if it'll stick to me. That's the point. I shall be the next to go.'

At once Maisie felt a sickening wave of terror, bringing back to her the moment when Walter first lost his job.

'Walter,' she said. 'You don't mean that really? You're such a good workman.'

'I might as well prepare you,' said Walter. 'All the other chaps left on now are pals of the foreman, or one of the bosses. That's what counts on this job; not good work.'

'Oh,' said Maisie. 'Why can't Mr. Truslove do anything? If only he could get you that job in Staedtler's.'

The next Friday Walter brought his money back from the flats for the last time. He climbed the stairs wearily, and gave Maisie the news in a dull, leaden voice. He was out of work again.

Maisie turned white when Walter told her; white and sick. It was worse now than it had been at first. She was more frightened. This time she had no feelings of calmness or hope. She looked at the blue and green oilcloth, which she had chosen so carefully—she looked at Walter's fine polished furniture.

The evening sun slanted into the room, and the bright sunlight broke up and danced in flashing points as tears filled her eyes. The room fell into pieces and vanished: and coloured circles, green and white and violet, raced away from her. The shouts of children came up from the streets below: from other places and times: from the time when she was a tiny child. The voices were distant, and dreamlike—but very loud and clear at the same time. She and Walter had fifty years more of life in front of them she thought. She saw dirty rooms and streets. She thought of bundles of rags, that cowered in doorways by night, and tottered, and moaned, and begged by daylight.

'Walter,' she cried. 'I can't stand it—I can't—I can't. What's going to happen to us?'

Walter stood and looked at her, his hands working nervously. His eyes filled with tears as they met hers.

'I'm sorry, Maisie,' he said. 'I'm no go, I'm afraid. I don't seem to be no use to you.'

Maisie dropped on to the bed and broke into a passion of crying.

'I'm thinking of our baby. We ought never to have started the baby—I knew it was wrong. People like us didn't never ought to have babies;

never; never. Isn't there anything I can do to stop it?' She went on weeping uncontrollably. Walter stood by her. Once or twice he put out his hand, and rested it on her shoulder or head for a moment.

After a long time a knock came at the door. Walter opened it and the landlady, who lived in the basement of the house, handed him a letter. It was addressed to Walter in typewriting. He opened it and stared at it for some time, then he began to talk very quickly to Maisie.

'Look,' he said. 'Look! That'll show us not to give up hope. Look what's come—a letter from the Staff Controller at Staedtler's. It says they are interested in particulars they have heard of me from Mr. Truslove, and from my late employers. I'm to go for an interview to-morrow morning.'

By dinner time the next day Walter was back home again, and they had engaged him.

'It seems too good to be true,' said Maisie. She laughed as she set the steaming dishes before him—and sat down herself. 'A job at Staedtler's. Well, that's one thing that will never go wrong.'

'You're right,' said Walter. 'It can't. All these building jobs are so risky and uncertain. Staedtler's is safe. This is a real job for life.'

Inside her Maisie felt the terror go right away to the very back of her mind. Warmth and sunlight filled her now, and pictures of family scenes with children and steady money coming in every week.

'I suppose you won't be working at carpentering at all now,' she said. 'Staedtler's make cycles and light cars, don't they?'

'Oh, that's a very small part of Staedtler's,' said Walter. 'They wouldn't have gone far on that. I shall be working in the main works, you see.'

'Well, what will you be making?' said Maisie.

'Didn't you know?' said Walter. Staedtler's is a munitions firm.'

WE WERE LOVERS TOO

When Jacqueline kissed him she always shut her eyes. The lashes lay dark against her cheeks, giving just the faintest flutter as if her eyes might open. He watched the tremulous pulse in her neck, and the tumble of her dark hair as it fell on the ground; the lovely black lustre curled against the leaf-mould, with ash-coloured twigs and dried ghost leaves clinging to it.

She put her bare arms round his neck; one round his neck under his open shirt, the other across his back gently drawing him closer and closer till the warmth of her body flooded him through and through. His limbs felt soothed and weightless, as if they were tassels of weed borne out in a flowing pool. The leaves and twigs, interlacing high above his head, moved gently with whisper voices, and diamond points of sunlight came sparkling through the green silence under the boughs.

He watched the trembling pulse in her throat and in her temple, and the soft flood of colour that spread rose-like under the transparent shell of her skin.

Suddenly Jacqueline opened her eyes and looked at him.

'You're staring at me,' she said. 'Have you been staring at me all the time?'

Jacqueline sat up. She brushed the twigs and

leaves from her lap, and began to comb her hair and powder her face.

'There,' she said. 'That's quite enough love-making. We must go for a walk. Let's walk round the hill, and then climb up to watch the sunset before we go.'

They found their way out of the tangle of trees and bushes that covered the hill-side and, taking a soft path, of trodden mast and leaf mould, came into an open field on the side of the hill. Butter-cups and long grass clustered round their ankles, and they gazed into the fresh, damp depths of the grass gemmed with flowers. The afternoon was now late and silent. Below their feet swayed the treetops and, beyond the nearer trees, the green and timbered landscape rolled away for mile upon mile in the golden evening light. Here and there the river flashed silver, and the spires and towers of the cathedral gleamed above the roofs of the town. The whole scene seemed to float in a golden, hazy light. Far off a train shrilled faintly and a plume of smoke threaded its line through the trees.

John looked at it anxiously.

'Do you know,' he said, 'that's the train I ought to have caught? I shan't get back till midnight now.'

'It doesn't matter,' said Jacqueline. 'Let's go right up to the top of the hill and forget all about it.'

They slowly climbed again through the trees and undergrowth, turning all the time to watch the sun as it sank. High up, they came upon the ruins of a tiny chapel lost and drowning in the verdure of the hill-side. They found a crumbling wall and buttress, an arch left hanging in the air, the stones locked and garlanded with green moss and creepers. A branching cable of ivy had wound through a single empty window, mingling its own traceries with the slender stone pilasters and trefoils.

They leant against the wall of this broken chantry facing westwards. The sun was falling now into a field of fire and flame. For a moment the whole sky seemed to be alive with jewels—rubies and rose diamonds. On every surface beside them, on grey stones, tree-trunks, on their own faces, shone answering gleams of gold. And the treescape spreading beneath their feet took vague and billowing shapes in the glow of coral light.

'Do you realize,' said John, 'that this is one of the very peak moments of our life? These few weeks, these few days, we've reached the main point of being alive at all.'

The glowing sky turned a faint shade colder as he spoke, a tinge of grey creeping into all the shadows.

'The moment is when you find each other,' he said. 'Then you marry, and from then on it's a gradual fading all the time; the edge being dulled . . . the colours fading. . . .'

'I can make nothing of middle-aged people,' he said. 'They seem to live on the level of stocks and shares and whiskys and sodas and indignant letters to *The Times*. But how can we ever sink to that?'

The light was fading faster and faster now. The jewels had vanished from the sky; the rosy light from the trees. The colour and the breeze grew cold. Soon nothing of the sun was left but a lilac stain and a few iron grey bars in the darkening air.

John suddenly began to see the night train journey before him. A lowering sadness fell in the air all about him, and a feeling of suppressed horror as the colour died from every leaf and blade of grass, turning from grey to still deeper shades. One or two swifts began silently darting, like black sprites, in the dusk.

'Come on,' he said, 'let's go.'

Jacqueline went on before him, and in a moment was lost to sight in the trees. Then as he turned to follow, he received a shock which made every nerve in his body recoil.

He saw that he was not alone; that for the last half-hour, as they had talked and kissed, they had been watched. Hidden in a corner of the broken building, on a pile of fallen stones, sat an old couple, unmoving, unspeaking.

Their clothes were as grey and colourless as the lichen in the dying light, their faces as lifeless horn or parchment; and deep in their eyes was the only sign of sentience, the look of grey and sunken age, of weariness redoubled upon weariness.

Matted and uncombed hair fell from under their caps. The man's hands, grey-white as wind-parched bones, were clasped round his knees; the woman, with bowed back and hands hidden in her sleeves, leant against him.

They sat huddled and derelict, like tattered rags bleached by a thousand suns and rains; lifeless as cold ashes in an empty house, as white skulls of sheep on a mountain side. Yet their eyes still watched him, and a night whisper seemed to eddy on the air, words shrill as a bat-thin squeak blown trembling high and far off on the wind . . .

'We were lovers too.'

John turned. For a moment he actually felt the young blood as something hot and ruttish, running in his veins, before it turned cold. Then he fled from the place.

I'LL SPOIL YOUR PRETTY FACE

"Don't be a b.f., I told him, 'haven't you ever heard of such a thing as doing it on your own doorstep? If you must go womanizing, have a little sense about it.'

But of course he didn't take any notice of me; didn't even listen. Have you ever known old Shottie listen to advice from anyone?

He just stood there, you know his way, on the balls of his feet with his head down, and glowered at me through his eyebrows, looking rather as if he was going to hit me.

'All right,' I said. 'You look as sullen as you damn well please. Being a champion boxer doesn't mean you aren't a b.f., and you ought to be grateful that I take the trouble to tell you so.'

Well, after that he just turned his back on me and walked up through the woods to the house. It was a wet day and the beech copse was sodden underfoot with mud and wet leaves, and everything was dripping and depressing; and I walked along feeling a bit foul and wondering if I'd really offended him.

When we got up to the house tea was ready, and Rachel (that's his sister) saw we'd been having a row—and I believe she guessed what it was about. Shottie wouldn't have any tea; he just went off to the gunroom by himself and started drinking whisky and soda—silly old ass.

After tea I had to go off and see a bloke; I was down there to look at some mining machinery, and had to spend a week or two at one of the collieries. That's why I took the opportunity of staying at Shottie's place.

That was only just after he'd come into it: and I remember thinking how funny it seemed, Shottie suddenly inheriting all that money and still going on as if he thought he was up against things.

On the way home I dropped into one of the local pubs, and I went to the public bar. I generally do on these trips. It's a good way of meeting men from the mines and getting some unofficial news and facts.

Well, I hadn't been in there long, and I was breaking the ice a bit, when an ugly sort of swine came up to me and said:

'Here—you? You're staying up at the Hall, aren't you?'

So I said I was.

'Well,' he said, 'tell your friend Sir Sholto Ayre—' at which he spat on the floor '—if he doesn't keep his hands off a certain girl, there's going to be trouble. I'll spoil his pretty face for him, so that girls won't want to look at him.'

I made no answer, because there wasn't any answer to make. That seemed to annoy him, and he put his face into mine and started jawing and jawing.

When he'd finished, I said:

'I don't know what the hell you're talking

about!' So he said: 'Oh, you don't? Well, you tell what I've said to him—I mean that little bastard up at the Hall—and tell him I'll spoil his pretty face: and I advise you to keep your nose out of our pubs, or I'll spoil yours, too.'

Well, after that things seemed a bit chilling in that bar, so I finished up what I was drinking and came out. When I got back to the house, I found Shottie had got himself more or less tight on whisky, and both Rachel and I were pretty fed up with him.

I wouldn't talk to him any more that night, anyhow.

But I nipped round to that pub and had a word with the landlord who was rather a good chap, and asked him what it was all about.

'It's serious all right,' he said. 'Take my advice, and make young Ayre keep off that girl. When a young fellow with all that money starts taking up with an ordinary girl like her, he means no good by it, does he?'

'It's not my affair,' I told him.

But he said. 'Well, make it your affair. This fellow Kirsten who was talking to you is a dangerous man. He's the sort that doesn't stop at anything, and I don't say I'd blame him, as she's his girl.'

'Who is this chap, anyhow?' I said.

'Well, I'll tell you one thing about him,' said the landlord, 'he's got a following round here. For the past three years he's been middle-weight champion at the Plew Valley Championships. He's the best boxer they've had for years, and if he meets your young friend Sir Sholto in the dark one night, he'll make mincemeat of him.'

'To hell with all these threats,' I said, and came away.

So I sat and talked to Shottie's sister in the drawing room, and she opened her heart to me a bit on the subject of Shottie: but we didn't get anywhere.

It did seem a bit needless, certainly, when he'd got everything he could ask for, arsing about like he did and trying to break his neck every time he went out hunting, and driving the Bentley about flat out, and all the rest of it.

For some reason he's always been up against it. He's not a talker, and it's damned hard to get hold of what he's driving at: but he tends to go on as if he thought the only things worth doing were the things the largest possible number of people would object to. God knows why—you know what he was always like.

Well, his sister told me a few things: their mother died when they were quite young: and I told her a few things: and she asked me if I wouldn't do something about it.

I said, 'My dear good girl, I agree with every word you say, but what can I do? The only thing is to leave him to himself.'

So things went on for a bit. I told Shottie about my meeting with Kirsten in the pub, and he just laughed and asked me if I'd got wind up: which was purely meant to annoy me.

Then one evening I saw this girl myself, and I must say I didn't altogether blame Shottie and I certainly did envy him.

I was coming up from the colliery one day—and it was a warm, lustful sort of spring evening. And as I came through the beech copse I saw Shottie and this wench standing together.

She was very yellow haired and pink and white—like Shottie himself—and there's no question she was a lovely piece of horseflesh. I'd better not go into a full description or I should get thrown out of here.

Have another pint, won't you? It's good stuff here.

Well, those two just stood still like a couple of statues looking into each other's eyes.

After a minute or so there was a loud crash of twigs and undergrowth, and Kirsten walked in on the scene. He'd obviously been looking for them. So I showed up too.

Kirsten barged straight in between them and aimed a blow at Shottie. Shottie caught him by the wrist. For a second things were pretty tense: then somehow or other the scrap faded out.

Kirsten put his face close to Shottie's and started jawing in his usual way:

'I'll spoil your pretty face,' he said. 'I'll find a way all right.'

Shottie said nothing: just looked at him. Then he suddenly turned and walked off.

And we found the girl had gone too.

'Damn swine,' said Shottie, and he repeated it at intervals as we walked along.

Well, I hoped this might sicken him off a bit; or at least show him that Rachel and I weren't just trying to annoy him. It certainly seemed to quieten him down, and for a few days he went about in a thoughtful way: and he made an effort to come out riding with us like a civilized being, and do other things with us, instead of going off by himself all the time.

A day or two later he suddenly said to me:

'It's a long time since I've done any boxing. I thought I'd have a shot at it again, so I've put my name in for some lousy local competition. You'd better stay over and be my second.'

'Right you are,' I said. 'What scrap is it?'

'It's the Plew Valley Championships: I believe it attracts quite a big entry round here. I thought I'd go for the light heavies, but I see I can just manage the middles.'

'I see,' I said. 'It's Kirsten you're after.'

The next day I asked my friend the landlord for a bit more information about these championships: and what he told me slightly shook me.

The Plew Valley Championships apparently got entries from about half a dozen counties in that part of the world—and they're a really big affair. In fact it's practically a professional meeting. For years they've been run by rather a shady set of people, and apparently they attract a terrific crowd of toughs. He said the whole town was expecting a rough house that night, and none of the decent men went near the place. And miners aren't exactly mollycoddles.

The landlord said: 'I hear your young friend the baronet has sent in an entry for the middles. Tell him to take my serious advice and keep out of it. Kirsten'll half-kill him if he ever gets to the finals.'

'Ayre is a damn good boxer,' I told him.

'Nonsense,' he said, 'what does he know about it? Schoolboy stuff. Kirsten's been at it for years. Ayre doesn't know anything. Besides, Kirsten'll have all his own pals round him. These championships aren't a garden party. Tell Ayre to keep out of it. I'm saying that for his own good.'

But still it was no earthly good my passing this on to Shottie: so I kept it to myself, and in due course the day came on—and the championships were due for seven o'clock in the evening at the Old Town Hall.

We got into the car, and Rachel would come too. I kept saying we ought to leave her behind. If there's one thing I hate, it's getting into a jam with a girl. But she was quite pig-headed about it, and Shottie seemed rather pleased.

But I'd have given a lot of money to have left her behind.

Well, as soon as we got inside the hall and I had a look round the room and the audience, I got a nasty kind of feeling that things weren't going to be quite plain sailing.

The Old Town Hall itself was enough to give you bad dreams. The distemper inside was pink: or it had been once. It was flaking off in a good many places. There were festoons of black grime and cobwebs on the walls. I shouldn't think the place had been cleaned or even touched since about 1840.

A few pictures of old boxing matches and Socialist get-togethers were stuck round: most of them tearing off too. The place was lit by naked gas jets with wire globes round them on brackets along the walls—and a big sort of bunch of hissing jets in the middle. The atmosphere was so thick and stinking that you could see a sort of dancing ring round every jet.

And the mob that was there: by God, you never saw such a set of bloody awful looking thugs in all your life: spitting about, and broken toothed, everyone shouting as if they were having rows with each other. They were pretty well packed all round the hall on backless wooden benches. I felt rather as if we'd got in among the baboons at the zoo.

Mind you, I'm not saying a word against a crowd of miners as such, because they're damn fine chaps: but these were the sweepings. What the landlord said was quite right: the decent men steered clear.

I can see that room when we first went in there as plainly as I can see you now. I don't know what old Shottie was thinking—but I got a touch of the horrors as soon as I got inside. I think it was the pink distemper as much as anything. Of course, Rachel was the only woman there, and I damn nearly told her to beat it; but I don't think it would have made any difference if I had.

Well, we didn't attract too much attention; anyhow, they all knew who we were and what we'd come for. There was a kind of adjoining small hall where the competitors went to be weighed in, and Shottie nipped in there while we stood at the back of the room: and in a few moments he came back and joined us. Everybody round us stared in a damned irritating sort of way, as if they were getting ready to have a bloody good joke at our expense. I had a good look at Rachel and saw she didn't like it much.

Well, after a while the scrapping began, and we saw one or two quite classy set-to's—a good deal of blood and not much boxing. The crowd got terrifically worked up and yelled out 'Punch him in the guts and in the liver', and so on: and they pretty well started scrapping among themselves.

In a way I wanted to laugh at the whole mob: but in another way I knew I'd got a nasty sort of wind-up in the back of my mind, and wished we were well out of it.

Here, have another pint, won't you? After all, we haven't met for five years, and God knows when we shall meet again. Where was I? Oh, yes—

We discovered from the programme that practically all the fights were finals. There were just one or two semi-finals. Shottie was in one of them, against a man rejoicing in the name of Dunk Bledlow. Shottie laughed a bit when he saw it down in print, and whispered in my ear, 'Bleed low, sweet chariot,' which seemed to strike him as a good joke.

There was no other semi-final in the middles, as there were only three entries and Kirsten had got a bye into the final.

The fight before Shottie's wasn't much good, and the crowd began to get a bit bored. Then, as soon as they saw what was next on the programme, a kind of rustle went all round the benches. I don't know what they expected to happen, but plainly they were all saying 'Now for it!'

Then the steward was calling out the names: 'Semi-Finals of the Open Middleweight Championship of the Plew Valley and District. In this corner, Dunk Bledloe—and in this Sir Sholto Ayre.' And as he said it, I got a sort of feeling of real funk, as if I was for it myself.

So we started pushing through from the back of the hall, and as I'd got to second Shottie, and we couldn't very well leave Rachel behind, she came with us: and you know what it's like when you get up on your legs in a public room and everybody's looking at you. Frankly, I'm not made for that sort of thing: the hustings aren't much in my line. We just walked through rows of damned ugly faces, most of which seemed to be laughing at us—and it made me feel bloody angry.

I managed to plunk Rachel down in a seat just by our corner, where she would be quite close to us : and then I got into the ring with Shottie and began to rub his legs and arms and so forth.

We were greeted with considerable booing and catcalls. I don't know why, but the general idea seemed to be that Shottie was just some pansy who thought he knew how to box, and was going to get eaten up by the local tiger in the shape of Mr. Dunk. There are always some coves about who think their own particular gang has got a monopoly of guts—and of course Shottie does go in for suede shoes and rather natty check coats : and his hair is all yellow and curly, and you can't but agree he hardly looks the tough nut he really is.

When they stood up in the ring there were various funny remarks in exaggerated sort of haw-haw voices, such as : 'Now let's have a little nice clean sport,' and 'I say, you chaps, you should see my straight left.'

Well, all this damn well infuriated me, as it probably did Shottie, and I began to put up some fervent prayers that he'd walk into Dunk and spread him all round the ring. At the same time I had no sort of idea what sort of class these chaps really were, and whether Shottie would be anything like good enough for him : and if he got beaten up I thought I'd blasted well challenge someone to a fight myself.

Then I took off his coat, and there were more

jokes : and there's no doubt Shottie did look like a lamb led to the slaughter in his white singlet and shorts and white socks.

Dunk got up, and he'd got nothing on but a pair of very tight black shorts : no vest. And his general appearance made Shottie look rather like a choir boy. He was red-headed : most of his hair had been shaved off, and he had the dumbest looking face I've ever seen—with a wide, silly sort of grin and a few blackened and broken teeth.

He had almost no neck and a very powerful pair of arms and shoulders : they often get like that in the mines. He looked as strong as an ox, but you could tell from looking at him he'd move like a slug, and he was obviously solid bone from the neck up.

'You'll fix him,' I said to Shottie. 'Keep off for a bit and konk him one or two quick ones from the distance, and see what his guard's like.'

Shottie didn't say anything : he just stood on the balls of his feet and began to tuck his chin in and look at Dunk through his eyebrows. And the light of battle came into his eyes—you remember the look.

I said, 'For God's sake hold your horses for a bit : he's a powerful looking lad. Get him a bit puffed and tied up first.'

But I could see I was wasting my breath. I don't know quite what was going on in Shottie's mind, but he was giving sweet Miss Adams for anything I said. I don't suppose he even heard it.

Well, then they shook hands and this fellow Dunk seemed to think he was sharing in the general hilarity at Shottie's expense. He gave a sort of zany-wise leer round at his pals, and started to prance about in a damn silly way as if he thought he were giving a humorous imitation of what Shottie's fancy style of boxing would be like.

But about a second after they'd shaken hands, Shottie gave him a terrific wipe on the jaw that seemed to come from nowhere it was so quick, and went clean through his guard as if he hadn't had one. And that took the grin off his face and pretty well rattled every tooth in his head.

And having done that, Shottie didn't waste a split second, but simply leapt on him and mixed it. And, by God, I began to sing a little song inside. It was fine. I saw in a flash what foul advice I'd given him in telling him to stand away and box: because as soon as he got to work it was perfectly obvious that Shot was much stronger than this fellow Dunk, and twice his class in every way.

And for about a minute he simply slammed that unfortunate silly lout round the ring so fast he hardly knew what was hitting him. He must have punched him about forty times in the guts and heart, and found time to uppercut him from close quarters till his head rocked. And I should think very likely he butted and bit him as well.

I've never seen him put up a more marvellous show. By God, it was grand. The whole crowd must have seen in a flash that they were getting a display of rough stuff that was classes better than anyone else had shown them.

After about a minute of this, Shottie got him up against the ropes and just about put him out; but Dunk managed to get into a sort of clinch and the referee pulled them apart and made them come out into the middle of the ring.

They stood facing each other, and there was quite a tense silence. Dunk was definitely groggy, and Shottie was just sort of pausing to take breath. Then Dunk's supporters began to pipe up, and someone booed and said Shottie had started before Dunk was ready. Then someone else said, 'He can't keep it up: he's soft. Slug him, Dunk. Knock his bloody teeth out.'

Well, that seemed to revive old Dunk a trifle, though he looked pretty green; and a faint glimmer of intelligence passed over his face: Shottie just stood on the balls of his feet with a slight spring in his knees, and looked almost as if he'd gone to sleep. So Dunk let out a wet sort of lead with his left—and as he did so, I knew exactly what was going to happen, because I'd seen Shottie do it before. He didn't step back, but whipped forward, letting Dunk's left go over his shoulder; and he loosed a terrific right hook into his heart, which Dunk lumbered right into.

I can tell you that's a most unpleasant blow of Shottie's, because he's done it to me: and it makes you wonder when your heart's going to start beating again.

Well, it shook Dunk to his foundations, and he doubled up over the blow ; and as he did so he got a terrific jab upwards from Shottie's left, and he began to stagger back. And as he went, Shottie let out the most marvellous and fizzing right swing you ever saw. By God, it was a peach. His fist started from the ground somewhere and travelled so fast you couldn't see it, and it caught Dunk on the jaw with every ounce of Shottie's soul and guts behind it.

It made a lovely, juicy sort of 'klop' that you could hear all over the hall—and Dunk sailed into the air. His heels went off the floor, and the first part of him to hit it again was the side of his head : and the crash shook the whole platform. Shottie didn't even take the trouble to look at him. He simply walked straight back to his corner.

Dunk absolutely passed out : you never saw a man in such a state of pulp. He was just a boneless lump of flesh till the counting was over. Then they dragged him to his corner and poured water on him and gave him brandy, but he flopped about like so much dead meat : and presently they dragged him away to the back of the hall and got to work on him there : but all they got out of him were some howls and barks like a sea-lion. I heard after he was concussed for days.

Meanwhile Shottie's win was received at first in grim silence : by the time it was announced, he'd got his coat on again and had climbed out of the ring and sat down beside Rachel without a hair out of place. I don't think he'd been hit once.

Presently someone broke the silence by saying: 'Well done, Ayre—show us some more.'

Then some sportsmen of the other faction began to yell and catcall—God knows why—and others shouted back, 'Well done, Ayre,' and there seemed to be every chance of a free fight all round us.

It died down again after a while, only some lousy idiot kept saying: 'You wait for Kirsten—he'll spoil your pretty face.' Shottie never batted an eyelid the whole time: he only turned to me once and whispered: 'Just you wait: I'll knock his jaw off,' which was undoubtedly the right spirit.

'Cheer up,' I said to Rachel. 'We'll soon be out of this now.'

She didn't say anything: just went on staring in front of her with a white face.

There were one or two more scraps, which seemed pretty tame. You know after you've been watching Shottie box everyone else seems to do it in slow motion. It was pretty evident the crowd were waiting for Shottie and Kirsten to come on. That was going to be the big spot in the evening. There was a kind of atmosphere of waiting in the air.

I hate waiting. I hate that sort of waiting where you're in for something and you've just got to muck round waiting for it to start. I just sat staring at the floor.

Let's have another pint of this four K, shall we?

It's good stuff. I wish old Shottie were here now. Cheero.

When it was our turn again, a hush fell all over the hall—quite a deadly hush. And Shottie and I got up and went to our corner. And Kirsten got up and went into his. And as I stood up in the ring and looked round at all those sweaty faces goggling up at me in the smoky air, and the rings round the gas jets, I had one of those damned queer feelings that it had all happened before.

And the faces and the room seemed to go all comic and far away like dolls, and the referee's voice suddenly stopped.

And the whole of my life and everything else I'd done seemed to vanish, and I felt I'd been standing there for years and years waiting to see Shottie through this business. Whatever it was had happened before, I'm dead sure I'd been in it with Shottie : that was the strongest feeling of all.

Then of course everything suddenly rushed back again, and I was back in the corner rubbing Shottie's arms and legs, with the shouting and noise all round me. He didn't say a word but was peering over my shoulder at Kirsten all the time.

There wasn't any funny stuff from the crowd this time. When the two of them got up, there was a dead silence. Kirsten looked far more like a fighter than this other fellow, Dunk. He wasn't so straight and well made all over as Shot : he was more of a hairy ape type. But he had the hell of a pair of shoulders and a long reach, and you could tell he was going to be pretty nippy.

One or two voices shouted, 'Come on, Kirsten—smash him up—show us what's inside him,' and soon there was quite a lot of shouting again. The referee waved for silence—and suddenly the whole mob started yelling madly : just yelling and yelling.

I think that without quite knowing what it was all about, they felt at last they'd got the very man in front of them—the owner of the land. The very chap who'd been sending them down the mines and sweating them for generations : and at last they'd got the chance of seeing one of their own crowd beat him up.

While this was going on, Shottie and Kirsten were just standing glowering at each other behind the referee's back, and I could see they were both beginning to breathe hard at each other. And they damn nearly went for each other there and then.

Then the shouting stopped, and the referee got his stuff in, and I nipped out of the ring and they were off.

And from the very first second that scrap was like nothing I've ever seen before or since. By God it was a shambles. It wasn't boxing at all : it was just a couple of bloody wild animals trying to kill each other.

The whole of the first round was just a sort of blur of the two of them, charging each other again and again. Butting each other : wrestling and slogging in clinches. And occasionally getting away from each other and exchanging slam for slam without the faintest attempt at guarding.

I've never seen fighting like it—and the crowd fairly got on its feet and roared. And they swayed about and lurched round the ring—and the shouting sort of swayed up and down with them. There was plenty of blood almost from the moment it started ; only you couldn't see whose it was.

When Shottie came back to me at the end of the round, I said : 'For God's sake ease off and box a bit : you can't keep that up.'

He took no notice, so I tried again while I was rubbing him.

'What the hell's the good of going on like a small boy who's lost his temper, and forgetting you're a bloody fine boxer ? Why don't you use your brains a bit ? This isn't a display of bag punching—it's a fight. You've got to win. If you go on like this he may get a lucky clip in and finish you off.'

But I was only wasting my breath. As soon as the bell went he sizzled out of his corner and rushed at Kirsten—and they began again. They were both landing terrific smacks every few seconds, and neither of them seemed to take the faintest notice.

Before very long they were both spouting blood, and with so much hitting and holding it got all over their faces and chests and arms—and there still seemed to be plenty to splash about the ring. And all the crowd were yelling their heads off.

When Shottie came back for the second time, he was just one gory mess, and he was panting for breath. I washed him up a bit, and saw one of his lips had been cut to ribbons against his teeth and was beginning to swell up like a muffin: it just streamed blood all the time. But apart from this he seemed all right. His zephyr had got almost torn off, so I took it away.

'Look here, you damn fool,' I said. 'Pull yourself together and fight sensibly.'

'Shut up, you sod,' he said, and they were off again.

But that sort of pace couldn't last, and about half-way through the next round they died down quite suddenly and began to circle round each other.

I saw that Kirsten was bleeding from the mouth and nose just as badly as Shottie, and also seemed to have a place laid open on his cheek. They fell to a bit of real boxing and both landed some snorters: by the end of the round they were plastered with blood again all over their chests and arms.

In the next round things weren't so good. Shottie's work began to lack sting—he'd pretty well done himself in. Kirsten was a damn fine boxer as well as a tough nut. What's more, he was about five years older than Shottie and had lashings more experience. He was up to all the tricks, and had an answer all ready for everything Shottie tried on him.

Shottie got slower and slower, and Kirsten was

swinging them in pretty regularly: really ugly bangs, that made Shottie rock on his feet. I could see he was getting worn down.

Then Shottie tried on the very same thing he'd finished off Dunk with, which wasn't too clever of him, because Kirsten had seen how it worked.

Kirsten led strongly with his left, and Shottie ducked forward and landed the right hook to the heart all right, but his left uppercut which followed went astray because Kirsten saw it coming, and it was Shottie that was left off his balance with his guard nowhere; and he got a quick cross over to the head that sent him down flat, and he just grovelled, and for a moment I thought he'd been outed.

But he got up at eight or nine and began to grope about in a pretty blind sort of way: he was half knocked out, but standing up, and he'd scraped an eyebrow on the floor so that a loose flap of skin started dangling over one eye and the blood got into it.

I thought it was just about all up—and a roar came up from the crowd to Kirsten to finish him. And Kirsten went after him, and Shottie just covered up and got beaten round the ring amid shouts of applause. It was pretty foul.

I was praying for the end of the round—but it seemed to drag on and on. Then Kirsten caught him in the corner and let swing an uppercut that was obviously meant to finish him off. But it just missed his chin and went ploughing into his teeth and mouth. It made me sick to see the fist go squelching into Shottie's mouth, which was cut to pieces already.

He lurched forward, and I saw clots of blood coming from his mouth. He went down on all fours. The bell rang, and I went and dragged him back to his corner.

One of his front upper teeth was pretty well gone. The gum was lacerated and the roots of the tooth were protruding through. I told him what it was like. He couldn't speak very intelligibly, but he told me to take it out. I got hold of the tooth with my thumb and forefinger and gave a lug—and it came away with a lot more blood, and Shottie gave a yelp.

'Let's chuck it,' I said. 'You can't go on.'

Shottie mumbled something or other—I could hardly hear what—but I gathered he was calling me names: so I cleaned him up with cold water. And back he went—pretty rocky. I wanted him to stop like Hell.

Let's finish this beer up and have another one, shall we? It's pretty good stuff.

Well, I tell you, when I saw Shottie standing up and going back again with that mouth of his, and his lips like blankets, and his whole face just battered and pulped, and wobbly on his legs—my heart went out to him.

You know that funny gesture he has, as if he were trying to pull up his shorts with his boxing gloves on? He kept doing that—I'd seen him do it so often—and I remembered him boxing other kids when he was about twelve. I wanted him to stop.

I had a look at Rachel, and I saw she was bracing her throat and mouth.

This was the fifth and last round, and I thought Kirsten has more or less fulfilled his promise of spoiling Shottie's face for him: at any rate for the time being.

But Kirsten wasn't looking too bright himself. He was getting pretty weak: and I think he'd lost heart because he hadn't put Shottie out in the last round. They leant on each other a fair amount, and there was a lot of weak clinching—and I began to pluck up and think Shottie would make it a draw after all.

And Shottie rallied a bit and caught Kirsten the most unholy wallop which sent him up against the ropes—and I sent up a cheer all on my own. A second or two later Shottie stumbled and overbalanced, and went down on all fours: then, as he was getting up with one knee and hand still on the ground, and no pretence of a guard — Kirsten slammed him full in the face as hard as he could, and sent him rolling over on his back. It was a deliberate foul.

There was just a yell—a total uproar. A second later and there were a dozen individual fights going on all over the room. I got into the ring.

The referee was trying to push Kirsten back,

and Shottie was on his feet again. Then Kirsten's pals swarmed into the ring and pulled the referee away.

'Let them fight it out!'

That's what they started shouting through the general turmoil.

Some of the crowd objected, but they got shouted down. 'Let them fight it out!' was being yelled from every part of the room. And a crowd of people collared the referee and me and lugged us out of the ring.

After that it was—oh, God, it was beastly. It became a sort of nightmare: only a nightmare that you're wide awake in. Just those two going on and on, both of them half conscious and half mad with what they'd had already—and the crowd yelling and yelling. From time to time the other seconds and I would watch our moment, and grab our men and bring them round again. That's about what it came to.

Shottle just knew he'd got to go on. There was just enough of his brain left for that. But he was simply beaten to a pulp. They'd both just got strength to go in and make it and each other a bit worse—and the crowd loved it.

Then the whole thing got more blurred. Gloves came off: accident at first, I suppose—and soon they were rolling about fighting with bare hands. Like animals. It was filthy. And the crowd shouting all the time.

I've seen those chaps stage dog fights just the

same way. They set a couple of dogs at each other till they're just about dead. It's not till they've got an eye chewed out or a leg broken that they begin to like it. Just imagine that with a couple of human beings.

At last they began to get tired of it and there were one or two shouts of 'Stop it—that's enough!' The seconds got into the ring and began to try and end it. I saw Kirsten rushing at Shottie in a last flicker of fight.

And then suddenly the lights went out.

Every one of those damn stinking gas jets simply vanished. And the place was so black after the lights you couldn't see an inch, and I was dragged out of the ring.

And in the darkness somebody gave a scream. A high-pitched scream that went on. It was Shottie's voice; and a lot of other noises—choking.

I wondered if I was going mad. I couldn't see a thing. Someone got his arms round my neck and I began fighting. People were trying to get me on the floor. And something was still going on in the ring; I could hear the noises.

Then I got hold of a stool and began hitting round with it in the dark. I felt it hitting heads. Then I thought of Rachel and shouted for her. The darkness gradually began to go grey, and I got my back to the wall at the side of the room. I don't know how long it went on—five or ten minutes, I suppose, but in my memory it seems as long as five years. Then a man started lighting the gas jets with a taper: and when people could see, the whole mob just froze stiff.

This is what had happened. Kirsten had got a razor from one of his seconds; they use 'em in those parts. It was all planned out beforehand. And the lights were put out as they gave it to him. And he had slashed it in Shottie's eyes and face.

That's why Shottie screamed. But he never put his hands to his face: that's what everyone else in the world would have done, I suppose. He'd got his hands on Kirsten's neck: I told you they'd got their gloves off.

I don't know whether Shottie knew what he was doing. Perhaps he was just waiting in the darkness and clutching—clutching on to anything. It gave him a maniac's strength. He drove his fingers through the flesh in some places.

As the lights went on one by one, that's what we saw—Kirsten didn't move.

When we got Shottie away he just collapsed. I found Rachel after a bit, and we got him home in the car. That part's all a blur: I can't remember.

Next day we heard that Kirsten wasn't dead. They'd worked on him for an hour with artificial respiration, and got some life into him at last. A chap like that takes some killing.

Shottie got over it more or less. He can see a bit with one eye; the other's absolutely dished, and his face is a pretty nasty sight. You'd get a shock if you ever met him. I see plenty of him. He was always my greatest friend; besides he's my brother-in-law now. I sometimes think he's gone a bit crackers since that night.

Yet in a way Shottie's got the laugh: in a way. Kirsten married that girl soon afterwards. She had a kid almost at once; a boy. And now that kid's about four or five there's no doubt that he's Shottie's child. Not an atom of doubt. He's got Shottie's face, you see. Kirsten didn't get rid of it after all.

It's a damned awful business. I can't ever talk about it till I'm fairly tight. Well, they're slinging us out of here now. It's getting late. Good-bye. Good-bye. Good-bye. . . .

BEES HAVE WARS, TOO

'Here's the honey for your mother, Harry,' said old Mr. Daintry. 'Mind you get it home safely. Tell her it's my heather honey—the very best there is.'

'Thank you very much.'

'Like to come down the garden and see the bee-hives?'

Harry nodded, and Mr. Daintry led the way out of his cool stone flagged hall, and into the glare of the lawn beyond.

The garden was drunk with the summer sunlight. Hardly a breath stirred to mingle the scents of jasmin, myrtle, and lime blossom, that hung in heavy coils on the air. The sun was so strong it was hard to keep your eyes awake.

And over everything, invisibly weighting the limbs, a web of sound was spun—the bee-voices: the innumerable bee-voices, rising, falling, dragging like a silken net at the nodding heads of the flowers.

As they walked towards the gigantic lime tree, the bee-voices swelled to an orchestra. Then they followed a path by a stream, and the noise grew fainter but still rose and fell sweetly in the distance.

'You've never seen hives at close quarters or watched bees at work, I suppose?' said Mr. Daintry.

'No.'

'It's a wonderful study,' he went on, leading the way slowly along the stream. 'Men have always philosophized about bees—even Aristotle. You know your Georgics of course much better than I do.'

He began to quote Latin, making a gentle murmur of sound, quite meaningless to Harry, save that it was low and drowsy and pleasant.

They came now to a place where the stream took a divided course: it wandered indolently in two branches for a hundred yards, and then joined again, 'eaving a small island of lush-grass and meadow lowers—a green inner bower, it seemed, of the summer itself. They went over a small, steep wooden bridge to the island. The dead hush of noonday was over everything and in the silence Harry felt suddenly there was a threat—a hint that something would happen.

They saw a bee crawling in the grass, whirring its wings without flying. It climbed a grass blade, as if to launch itself in the air—but fell floundering down.

'I don't quite like the look of that,' said Mr. Daintry.

'What's wrong?'

'There's a bee disease called acarine disease, and that's one of the symptoms. But we've had none at all this year.'

Mr. Daintry went on watching the bee.

'That's not acarine,' he said. 'This bee's been injured.'

Harry looked at the bee. He felt a pang, that

out of thousands of happy bees, this one should be drawling helplessly with broken wings.

'I suppose it'll die,' he said.

'Hush,' said Mr. Daintry. 'Listen—Listen.'

He waited for a moment in complete silence, holding his hand in the air.

'Listen,' said Mr. Daintry. 'Robbers.'

He quickly led the way close to the hives—a little township of white houses in the grass.

'Now,' said Mr. Daintry, 'listen to the humming. Do you hear the different note?'

Harry knew now what he meant. The bee voices, so drowsy and peaceful before, had changed. The bees were making a noise that he had never heard bees make. It was angry, and vicious.

'I see where the trouble is,' said Mr. Daintry. He went to a hive at some distance from the rest. The hive, which was like a white doll's house, was surrounded with hovering angry-sounding bees.

'Yes,' said Mr. Daintry. 'Robbers—and they're none of my bees either.'

'How can you tell?' said Harry.

'Look. You see the ones that fly straight in: they're the defenders. They're my bees. There goes one,' he said. 'There's another.'

Harry nodded.

Every few seconds a new arrival came up, and with a steady purposeful flight passed into the entrance of the hive.

'They're coming in fast,' said Mr. Daintry. 'The attackers are the ones that hover about.

They're bigger than my bees, and they're more yellow.'

'I'm on *your* bees' side,' said Harry. 'Will they drive them off?'

'I hope so.'

They watched in silence.

'I never knew bees went to war,' the boy said. 'What's it about?'

'Honey,' said Mr. Daintry. 'Bees fight over honey, men over money.'

'Do you mean the attacking bees are trying to take the honey from this hive?'

'That's it.'

For the first time they saw one of the yellow attacking bees meet a dark defender on the entrance board of the hive. Suddenly the two bees grappled and there was a spurt of buzzing. With a faint thrill of horror Harry saw their stings plunging at each other. In an instant the defending bee was dead, and its corpse slipped to the ground. The attacking bee crawled a little way, then it, too, fell dead.

'Why don't these beastly attacking bees take their own honey from the flowers?' he said. 'I never knew they went for other bees like this.'

'They do sometimes,' said Mr. Daintry. 'But it's very rare until late in the year: they usually wait till flowers are becoming scarce. Sometimes you just get a vicious strain in the bees. Perhaps I dropped a piece of comb near this hive: that may have incited them.'

'I wish we could do something,' said Harry.

'We can do a few things to help,' said Mr. Daintry. 'Let's try.'

He took Harry to his stables, which were empty save for one old mare, and told him to collect some handfuls of hay. They returned to the hives and the angry note was even more insistent. Everywhere the alarm was being trumpeted.

The yellow robber bees were growing bolder and bolder. Attacked and attackers met at the entrance. Several corpses lay before the hive, and wounded and mutilated bees crawled helplessly.

'Take care, Harry,' said the bee-keeper. 'I shouldn't go too near. They're all in a state of frenzy.'

He packed the hay loosely round the entrance to the hive. This gave no great difficulty to the homing bees, who knew the entrance was there and, after a few seconds' hovering, found their way in. But it baffled the attackers, who buzzed all round the hive, or became entangled in the hay.

It was now late in the morning. Harry took the pot of honey that Mr. Daintry was sending to his parents, and went home to lunch. Directly he could leave, he set off again to see how the battle was shaping. He went by the fields and climbed into Mr. Daintry's garden from the back, not liking to disturb him again.

Round the hives there was an angry thrum of noise, loud and unceasing. Like hordes of enemy aeroplanes the robber bees droned up to the attack.

He went close to the hive, and saw the battle had reached a new phase. The robbers had broken down all Mr. Daintry's defences. The hay had been dispersed by their thrusting bodies and lay scattered. The robbers found the way in easily now.

And the robber bees were coming out of the hive too. A steady stream of them was crawling from the hive entrance unscathed and flying off. These, he thought, must have all plundered successfully.

In the meantime the fear and agitation of the attack had spread to the other bee colonies on the island. Excited bees thronged the alighting board alert to spot enemies, running to new arrivals or darting at robber bees in the air. There was no honey gathering : they crawled and flew and crawled again, and round every hive wheeled a drumming horde of bees.

'Don't stand so near those hives, Harry,' said Mr. Daintry's voice suddenly behind him. 'Don't you see how excited they are : you may get badly stung.'

Mr. Daintry approached the hives himself.

'This is bad,' he said at once. 'This is very bad. I never thought we'd get an attack like this. See them flying off with the honey, too.'

'What can you do now?'

'Nothing for the moment. But the afternoon's beginning to close in now, and the worst's over. They're mostly going now, not coming.'

They turned away from the hives, leaving the

dead and dying bees on the ground. The air was as hot as ever : the whole garden was drugged and drooping with the heat.

'I told the owner of those bees he was going to have trouble,' said Mr. Daintry. 'These are cross-bred Italian bees—and they're given to this sort of thing. Italian bees are very peaceable on the whole but they're very queer when they're crossed. Last year he introduced a new queen to one hive, and she's produced a bad strain. You see a queen bee mothers a whole colony in less than a year, so a bad heredity spreads quickly.'

Harry nodded, after a while said : 'I'd no idea you had bees of different nations. I thought they just belonged here.'

'Far from it,' said Mr. Daintry. 'We have all the nations of Europe in bee-land and some Asiatics and Africans too. There are the Carniolans and Italians : bees from Switzerland, Austria, Cyprus, Greece, Syria, Egypt, There's the Banat bee of Hungary, the Ligurian bee, the Punic bee of North Africa, the Holyland bee—I daresay that's all. Quite a league of nations, isn't it?'

'Yes,' said the boy. From far off they could still hear the buzz of the warriors in the heat of the afternoon.

'And when robber bees attack a hive like this, do those other bees, in the nearby hives, ever go to their rescue and fight for them?'

'No,' said Mr. Daintry. 'I've never heard of it. They only fight if their own hive is attacked. But an attack of robbers has a nasty effect all round. You see how angry and dangerous all the bees become. When a fight like this is going on sometimes the other colonies begin attacking each other : just from sheer infection of excitement. Then there's a very pretty pickle.'

He quoted some more Latin.

'I hope your bees will be left alone to-morrow,' said Harry. 'I don't think they have a fair chance against those yellow ones. They're much bigger.'

'There are more of them, too,' said Mr. Daintry. 'I'm afraid that's rather a weak colony. Well, good-bye, Harry, good-bye. I don't think they'll worry us any more to-morrow.'

That evening Harry found the noise and the image of the warring bees continuing in his head. He dreamt of bees—black and yellow and furry.

The next day he was unable to visit the hives till the afternoon. As soon as he was free, he went straight to Mr. Daintry's garden. There was no sign of Mr. Daintry.

But he found that Mr. Daintry had been wrong, utterly wrong, in saying that the enemy would not attack again. Fighting had been going on all day : the attackers, even more determined, streamed into the hive. The smaller defending bees seemed to be growing more and more feeble in their resistance. The other bees still buzzed angrily and restlessly round the hives.

Over all the garden hung the same dreamlike heat and stupor. Harry was obsessed with a strange feeling of distance. From a far-off world of garden loveliness he watched violence and death in the bees' world. Had they feelings? Were they suffering, despairing, every moment before his eyes? A veil of brilliance hung over the scene : a veil of youthful vision, at once making the colours brighter, but the meaning yet more dark and mysterious.

Several times he wandered in the fields and came back. At length Mr. Daintry came home from a distant visit and joined him. He inspected the hives at once.

'I never expected this,' he said. 'I'd no idea they'd come back. I could have moved the hive into a secluded place and sprayed something round it last night. Still, it's too late now.'

'I'm afraid the enemies are winning,' said Harry.

'Yes,' said Mr. Daintry, scratching his chin. 'They'll capture the whole colony if we aren't careful. Watch closely and you'll see some of my bees are flying off with the others.'

They watched in silence.

'Are they running away?' Harry asked.

'Worse still,' said Mr. Daintry. 'They're *deserting*: going over to the enemy and taking the honey with them. It shows the other bees have pretty well mastered them.'

An hour or two later, in the cool of the evening, Harry, with a veil over his face, helped Mr. Daintry move the attacked hive to an outhouse, in an entirely different part of the garden. Mr. Daintry quietened the bees by blowing a streak or two of smoke into the top of the hive. He lifted out one or two combs.

'I think the queen's all right,' he said, 'But we've lost half our bees and a great deal of honey.'

He replaced the parts of the hive.

'I shall leave them here for a little while,' he said. 'They ought to be perfectly safe here for a few days. If the robbers found them again to-morrow, the whole colony might be wiped out. As it is they've lost their summer's work.'

At his words a picture crossed Harry's mind. He thought of the unhappy defeated bees crawling among their ruined combs and galleries : their hive half empty : their workers killed : their cells sacked.

'I *hate* those enemy bees,' he said to Mr. Daintry. 'I hate them. They come and attack yours for no reason—and they're just allowed to get away with it. It's a shame.'

Mr. Daintry smiled.

'No, Harry,' he said. 'We can't allow that : or the peaceful bees would never be safe. I've had a word with the owner of these bees already, and to-morrow that colony of robbers is going to be destroyed : every single bee. It's the only thing to do.'